# PEN HUSTLAS PUBLICATIONS

## She's HOPE WORTH IT 2

### SOME GHETTO SH*T

# NIKI JILVONTAE

# I Hope She's Worth It 2: Some Ghetto Shit

By: Niki Jilvontae

I Hope She Was Worth It 2: Some Ghetto Shit
Story
-A Novel Written By-
Niki Jilvontae
Copyright © 2016 by Pen Hustlas Publications
Published by Pen Hustlas Publications
Join our Mailing list by texting PenHustlas to
95577
Facebook: Niki Jilvontae

Cover Design: Tina Louise
Editor: Venitia Crawford

# Table of Contents

Synopsis

Dedication

Acknowledgements

Chapter 1

Chapter 2

Chapter 3

Chapter 4

Chapter 5

Chapter 6

Chapter 7

Chapter 8

Chapter 9

Chapter 10

Chapter 11

# Synopsis

Love is blind... some love can be quick. Love can endure the tests of time, or lead you to Some Ghetto Sh*t. This is a lesson many have to learn the hard way and Quaderious Jones is no different. The tale of Quatty continues in this sequel as he begins to wonder if any woman is worth all he has gone through. With Pooh still alive and not giving up and secrets surrounding his relationship with Tinka hanging over his head, Quatty is put to the test. More murder, secrets, heartache, jail time, and lies are in his future along with some ghetto shit he can't escape. Come on this turbulent ride as Quatty continues to ask himself... Is She Worth It?

## Dedication

I dedicate this book to my Liveme.com fans. Thank you all for the love and motivation each day!!!

## Acknowledgements

As always, I'd like to thank the Most High for this incredible gift. I'd also like to thank my family for their support along with my bestie boo love/beta reader Climaxxx. To my most loyal readers: Ciera Lawrence, MyRe Childs, and Cali Nicole... love you ladies. Major S/O to my mentor Shameek Speight and all of my TGP sister families RDP, PDP, MLP, LLP, MGP, and anyone else I may have missed...love y'all & let's get it. And special love and thanks to some of my Liveme.com Family: Kisses to my King Greg aka G-Man82, Jasmine, LS Jrock Knox, Bossinato72r aka Anthony, Young C paid, Petty Prince, Big Jackpot, Shoota290, my baby David Huckaby, Mr. Louisanna504, JW, Unlimited Breed, Miss Juicy D.O.C., Ghost, Lemon, & Jugg_&_Finessin.

# Chapter 1

I marched back into the house paranoid, tired, and mad as hell before I locked every lock on the door behind me and grabbed my 9MM out of the drawer in the table next to the door. I stood there and glanced at myself in the mirror for a second as I tucked the gun into the back of my pants.

"Is she worth it my nigga?" I whispered to myself as looked down and remembered the slip of paper from the box I still held.

I had never thought about whether or not Tinka was worth all the shit I was going through because I knew none of the shit that was happening was her fault. Pooh was just a crazy bitch who thought she owned me and could control everything I did, Tinka had nothing to do with that. If anything, all of the ghetto shit I was going through was my own fault for allowing Pooh to do the things she did for so long. I set myself up for the fuck up and I knew it, that was no one's fault but my own. However, even with that knowledge and the love I had for Tinka, I still found myself repeating that question as I mobbed into the living room. The ringing phones in the house continued to blare in my ears as I walked in.

"WHO THE FUCK CALLING." Ghost yelled as I stormed back past him and he peered up at me through the darkness.

My fucking mind was racing a mile a minute as I stormed over to the spider lamp by the couch, avoiding everyone's eyes in the room until I flicked the light on. Everybody was up and had their phones in hand when the light came on and I instantly met eyes with Tinka.

"What's going on Quatty?" she asked me with concern and anger on her face as she held her phone to her ear.

I shook my head like I didn't know as I quickly looked at Ghost like, *Nigga it's about to go down*, and he instantly knew what the look meant.

"What's going on is, that bitch ain't dead, but she damn sure will be." I said as I found my phone and keys before turning back to my niggas and they nodded.

I knew that was confirmation that they would follow through with what needed to be done should my sometimes soft ass fail to do it. That made me feel fucked up inside because I knew it was necessary. I knew when it came down to it, I couldn't actually kill Pooh unless I was given no choice. Even after all she had done to me and all those I loved, I still couldn't see myself pulling the trigger. My niggas knew that shit which is why they were ready for whatever…

Peedy and Ghost had been my best friends long enough to know my next move before I did. They knew I always had heart, but they also knew that I couldn't really harm a hair on that bitch head. I knew that shit too and hated it. I hated still caring about whether she lived or died but being able to cut a nigga down without a second thought. That was because none of those niggas I bodied on the streets have a tie to my heart like Pooh's rotten ass did. Killing them was no comparison to killing her. That was a fact I couldn't avoid and one I hoped would soon change, which is why I shook off those thoughts as I looked back at Tinka and continued to fill them in on what was going on.

"After that bullet to the gut last night, I know that ain't Pooh calling but what I do know is that she sent whoever it is. Some muthafucka left a box full of these muthafucking slips of paper on the porch." I said as I handed it to Tinka.

"That bitch ain't gonna give up until she gone so WE gotta make sure it gets done. It gotta be the right way though so I'm gonna sit on this for a minute. I know 12 looking for my ass by now anyway so laying low is imperative. In the meantime though, we got some business to handle my niggas." I said as I turned to Ghost and Peedy, and they jumped up and headed to the door.

"Damn baby." I said as I looked at Tinka and tears, nervousness and a little bit of guilt flickered in her eyes.

I wondered where that emotion was coming from as I stared at her beautiful ass, but I couldn't focus on that with all that was going. My heart hurt like a muthafucka to see her in so much pain because of me. I rubbed her stomach as she hugged me and kissed my neck while I inhaled her scent. I hated to tell her what I was about to say, but it was something that had to be said.

"Baby, I may have to do a little time behind this shit, but I'm gonna handle this bitch first. I gotta right my wrongs and end this once and for all. I'm sorry. I'm sorry for all of this. This shit all my fault. I love you though." I said as I looked back down at Tinka and I watched tears fall from her eyes.

I kissed her eyelids gently then her forehead before I turned and tried to walk away. Tinka grabbed my arm and whipped me around just as I got to the door.

"Quatty, wait. Don't go yet. I really need to talk to you. Baby, just don't go we can leave now and hideout. I don't want you to go to jail Quatty. Just stay and talk to me. This is really important." Tinka cried as I grabbed her and hugged her in my arms.

I didn't want to go either, but I had to go. I knew that shit was about to get ugly and I didn't want her to go through all of the death and destruction that was sure to come if I wasn't smart. I couldn't tell how shit would turn out with Pooh being all unpredictable and shit, so thinking two steps ahead was best. I needed to cover our asses if the police did come knocking so I wasn't falling for Tinka's *important talk* tricks.

"Look Tinka, I love you baby, but I got to go. This is something I have to do. I ain't about to get into shit right now, I promise. I just gotta get to the shop and cover our asses. Me and the boys need an alibi for last night so I got a homie that can fix up the tapes. You and Yada just stay here and wait for me to get back. I promise I'm not about to go nowhere I'm not coming back from. That's my word. We can have that talk the second I walk through the door. Aite?" I asked Tinka as I saw a flicker of relief flash in her eyes before she sighed and then kissed me gently on the lips.

I stood there and savored the sweet taste of her lips for a minute before I ran out of the house and hopped in my car. I glanced at her once more as she stood in the doorway with tears in her eyes while she rubbed her belly and I prayed I would make it back to her. I kept the image of her beautiful face in my mind as I pulled away from love and drove straight towards chaos. I pushed the medal to the floor as I whipped towards Tinka's shop in silence while my boys made phone calls and talked about what would have happen next.

I was in a daze as I drove until Peedy said that his hacker friend Josh would meet us there to change the date stamp on the tapes. I felt a bit relieved when I heard that because that was still one part of my plan I hadn't figured out. With that out of the way I got lost in my thoughts again until I heard them talk about cutting Pooh's fucking heart out to ensure she was dead. Those words stung a little, to my surprise, but I wouldn't let it register in my heart. I cut my emotions off and took on that numbness I only felt in jail to keep from stopping what I had to be done.

By the time we pulled up I was back in the I don't give a fuck Quatty mode, just ready to get the shit over with and back to Tinka. After a brief introduction with Josh at the back door, we all slipped into the shop and Josh got to work doing what he did best. He quickly accessed the company's security system and found tapes of us from weeks before. We all stood around and watched him work to change the time stamp on the footage of us working late into the morning in the stock room as Ghost fired up a blunt. I looked at that nigga like he had lost his mind until I smelled the loud he was smoking. I didn't want him smoking out baby's office but at that point, a little weed was the least of our concern. I guess that was Ghost's thoughts too because he suddenly shrugged and handed it to me.

"I know this ain't professional or apart of the norm and shit but right now nigga we well beyond the norm. All of us need something in our fucking systems to get through this shit." Ghost said as I nodded my head and Peedy and Josh agreed with what Ghost had said.

I hit the dope again as they talked amongst themselves and I let the high-grade cannabis do what it was supposed to do. I felt some of the tension and anxiety I was carrying start to disappear, the more I hit the weed. That didn't stop my mind from moving though and thoughts of jail and ending up dead popped in my mind as I handed the blunt to Peedy. He could see the fear in me as I tried to quickly look away but it was too late.

"You aite bruh?" Peedy asked me as I shook my head yes and lied to him and myself.

I wasn't okay, I was fucked up in the head and the nagging feeling in my heart told me shit was about to get worse.

"Maine, this system is a little bit more complicated than I thought. This gonna take a little longer than I initially planned." Josh said as the first rift in my plan damn near pushed me over the edge.

I couldn't even hide my disappointment and anxiety as I mobbed out of the room and slammed the door shut behind me.

"Damn, what's up with him?" I heard Josh ask from inside the office as I leaned on the door and closed my eyes while I tried to catch my breath.

"He good fool. Just work on that tape." Ghost said back to him.

The only thing was, a nigga wasn't cool, not at all. I was on the edge and ready to jump the fuck off. I needed that alibi for when the cops came knocking because I knew they would definitely be coming.

"What the fuck? What the fuck I'm gonna do? Think, nigga think?" I said to myself as I walked deeper into the store and tried to clear my mind so that I could find other solutions.

As soon as I stepped inside the store the smell of Tinka's perfume lingered in the air and caused the hard, callus side of me to soften a little. I walked around and stared at all of the pictures of her on the walls before I ended up on the stool behind the counter. I sat there and ran my fingers over the small picture of her sitting near the register as I told that voice inside of me what my heart already knew.

"Yes, she is worth it." I said to myself as I kissed my fingers and then laid them over Tinka's lips in the picture before I stood up.

Just then a small pink box with old childhood pictures on the outside and the words my memories written on the side of it caught my attention. I don't know why but the box intrigued me, probably because of the shit I had found in a box earlier. You would have thought that would have kept my black ass from opening it, but it didn't. My curiosity got the best of me as I bent over picked up the box and sat it on the counter. As soon as I opened it I began to regret my decision when I learned that it belonged to Tinka.

The box was filled with pictures, some from childhood and some more recent, and they all included Tinka and some dude. One picture in particular caught my eye and I damn near punched the cash register when I picked it up and glared at Tinka all snug in Dip's arms. Even though I knew she was engaged to him before me I still was mad seeing her with the nigga all hugged up and shit. He was the same nigga who damn near beat her to death and tried to take my life, so I didn't want to see her with him at all.

I started to rip that muthafucka up and erase his bitch ass from her memories like I had erased him from her life, but something told me not to. I didn't give a damn about her knowing I had found the secret box she hid from me at work. No, that wasn't why I couldn't rip it up. I couldn't rip it up because something in my heart said turn the picture over and when I did I knew why. Written on the back of the picture was the words, me and my first love, and it was dated only a week before Tinka and I met. There she was all cute with the same hairstyle she had when I met her in the club, boo'd up with that big bitch in his prison blues.

"What the fuck?" I whispered to myself as I sat back on to the stool and tried to let the shit I had just read sink in.

My mind went through a dozen scenarios as I sat there and held the picture in my hand. I couldn't figure out why Tinka had lied to me when she said she hadn't seen or talked to Dip since he went to jail. I knew that shit wasn't true when I had the picture right there in my fucking face. Anger filled my heart as I thought about how she had lied to me and wondered what else she hadn't been honest about.

I had put my all into our relationship from the start and even though shit had happened so fast, I thought she was the one. I was questioning all of that though as I sat there with the knife that stabbed my heart. I decided the only way to find out what was going on was to get it straight from the horse's mouth so I quickly took my phone out and dialed Tinka's number. After three rings, I started to get impatient but I wasn't about to hang up. I let that bitch ring three more times before Yada suddenly answered the phone, out of breath and flustered.

"Yo Yada, let me holler at Tinka. ASAP!" I said with coldness in my voice that made Yada stop her small talk before it began.

I heard her pause for minute as she walked through the house then the sound of Tinka heaving filled my ears.

"Yeah, Quatty, I don't think it's going to be possible for you to talk to Tinka right now because she sick as hell. I made us breakfast, she ate a little bit, and then she got sick. She been puking her guts out for about five minutes now, so I don't know what to tell you. I don't know if it's your baby or my horrible ass food, but what I do know is lil mama can't do no talking." Yada said as she laughed and tried to lighten my mood.

Her effort worked a little because I suddenly remembered my seed growing inside Tinka. I had forgotten about the baby in all the chaos so I tried to soothe my aching heart. It worked for a moment as I thought about the second chance we were getting after losing the first baby. However, when I remember the picture in my hand my anger crept back in again and I couldn't do shit to hide it.

"Aw yeah, well tell her as soon as she feels better she needs to hit me up. She right, we do need to FUCKING talk." I said before I hung up the phone and threw the picture back into the box.

"Maine, what the fuck?" I screamed out to myself in frustration as I kicked the box and banged on the table.

I couldn't believe I was in the same position again, at the crossroads of my life because of a bitch. I started to rethink whether Tinka was worth any muthafucking thing as I sat there and fought back my tears. That was the last thing I wanted to do, cry like a bitch because of a bitch, so I sucked that shit up and chose anger or hurt instead.

"Wasup bruh?" Peedy asked me as he suddenly appeared at my side and I shook my head.

"Maine bruh don't tell me nothing when you clicking out like a hoe on her period. Wasup bruh?" Peedy asked me and I went ahead and told that nigga the little bit that knew.

He listened as I talked and when I showed him the box with the pictures in it I watched the calm expression on his face change.

"Aite bruh, now I can see why you upset, but you know I wouldn't be yo nigga if I didn't tell you the truth. The truth is you need to wait and see what she has to say. Maybe what she had to tell you before we left has something to do with this shit. Now, I'm not saying it's right cause she violating by hiding the shit here after y'all been together for a minute and she could have told you this shit from the jump, but at the same time we just don't know bruh. You already on edge from the shit that happened last night and not knowing whether a muthafucka done snitched probably fucking with you too. That's why you need to slow down fool and just wait and see. She a good chick bruh. Don't make no irrational decisions." Peedy said as I shook my head and bit my bottom lip while I deeply exhaled.

I let go all of that anxiety and anger as I let my nigga's words sink in and tried to get rid of the nagging in my heart. I knew there was more shit to come and I probably wouldn't like it, but I decided to just wait and see.

"Aite bruh, you right. This shit just fucked up though. This Pooh bitch and her bullshit, losing a baby, possible jail time, and now Tinka may be fucking up too. That's just too much for one nigga to deal with my guy." I said to Peedy as he shook his head that he understood and fired up another blunt.

"I know the fuck it is, but that's why you ain't gotta deal with shit alone. We got you nigga." Peedy said as he reached out and gave me dap with one hand and handed me the blunt with the other.

"Now get yo ole sensitive thug looking ass up and let's go get this shit done." Peedy said as he pulled me up by my hand like he did in life and we walked back into the office.

By the time we got back into the room with Josh and Ghost I had pushed all that shit with Tinka to the back of my mind right along with the plan to kill Pooh. All I wanted to do was get my alibi straight and go spend as much time as I could with Tinka. I needed her to clear some shit up and I needed her loving before it was too late.

I tried to keep my mind off all of that as me and my boys chain smoked weed and ate snacks from the vending machines for damn near six hours while watching Josh work.

By the time he finally encrypted the code on the security system and changed the date on the tape to show all three of us there, it was almost eight at night and beginning to get dark. I felt twenty pounds lighter as we walked out the shop, paid, Josh, then got back into my car. I cruised back to our side of town with nothing but answers on my mind until my phone began to ring. I quickly answered it and Tinka's voice filled my ears as she asked me what was wrong.

"I just woke up baby. I called you as soon as I opened my eyes because Yada said when she talked to you earlier you seemed upset. Wasup? I would have called sooner but I was too sick. What is it though baby?" Tinka said as I sucked in my breath and held back what I wanted to say.

I wanted to yell out that she lied to me and ask her why she had a fucking box of memories she hid at work. Yeah, that scorned little bitch nigga inside me wanted to say all of that and some more but the real nigga wouldn't let me. I knew that was neither the time or the place to do that so I brushed off her questions.

"Don't worry about all of that, we'll talk when I get home. Do you want something to eat?" I asked her with a hint of malice in my voice that I was sure she caught on to.

I heard her gasp and suck in her breath before she answered my question. After she told me what her and Yada wanted to eat from Chilli's I quickly told her I'd see her in a minute and hung up without saying that I loved her. I still did, but I just didn't want to say it because my heart was so hurt. I couldn't help but to think she was still fucking off with the nigga before he died every time that picture popped up in my head. That was all I could think about as I drove to the restaurant, went inside to order us all some food, and waited for it to get ready.

By the time I got back into the car my boys had all of the plans in motion and I felt confident that my hell would soon be over. I kinda even forgot about the issue with the pictures of the Dip nigga until we walked into the house. As soon as we stepped inside and I saw Tinka all sad but glowing, curled up on the couch under my favorite blanket the memories started to fill my mind again. The only difference was I didn't feel angry anymore. Instead I felt sad and determined not to lose the best thing that had happened to me. That's why I pushed my hurt to the side as I took Tinka's food into the living room and sat beside her with a slight smile on my face. As soon as she opened her eyes and looked at me she sat up with worry written all over her beautiful, caramel face.

"Quatty baby, when did you get here? I just dozed off because my stomach hurting and nerves so bad. Somebody has been calling all day playing on the phone and shit. I was going to cut it off but I didn't want to miss your call. You sounded so upset the last time that we talked I almost thought you weren't going to come home. What's going on Quatty?" Tinka asked me as tears welled up in her eyes and I slid closer to her to wipe them away.

The last thing I wanted to do was put undue stress on her and risk the life growing inside, which is why I decided the bullshit could wait. All I wanted and needed was her love.

"Don't worry about that baby, we'll get into that later. Right now, all I want to do is make sure you and little baby are straight and soak up some of your loving. That's all I need." I said as I smiled at her and then kissed her gently on her lips.

Tinka couldn't hide her apprehension as she barely kissed me back and kept her sad eyes trained on mine.

"You sure baby because it seems like something was really fucking with you. I really need to tell you something though Quatty. It's something I really should have told you long ago but I was too scared." Tinka said as my heart raced and I blocked out her words.

I didn't want to hear that shit right then, really I didn't want to do anything but get inside of her warmness. I knew what my near future would hold and that didn't include pussy so I was ready to stockpile me some of that pink starburst before it was too late.

"Nah baby, not now. We'll have time for that. Let's just focus on us right now; you, me, and lil baby. Nothing else matters. Okay baby?" I asked her as I held her face in my hand and then kissed her deeply and passionately on the lips.

I felt the room move with that kiss and something tingle in my heart that told me nothing else did matter and she felt it too.

"Okay baby, later. I love you Quaderious." Tinka said with pain in her eyes as I kissed away the few tears that had escaped.

"I love you more Nicole, now feed my baby before I have to get you. You know that's a damn football player in there. The boy gotta eat." I said trying to lighten the moment and remove that look in Tinka's eyes.

It worked too because she instantly laughed and I saw that twinkle in her eyes that I loved. After that it felt like nothing had happened as we all sat in the living room and ate while watching reruns of the Dave Chapel show. I tried to enjoy the episodes I had missed but I couldn't sit still. Every minute I was up and looking out of the window, expecting 12 to bust down the door and take my black ass to jail. Around 11 pm Peedy, Ghost, and Yada left and I finally sat my ass down, exhausted and mentally drained. I held Tinka's head in my lap as she laid there quietly and listened to me breathe.

"Quatty, I don't know what I'll do without you. I know we've only been together a few months and we got into this relationship pretty fast, but somehow I feel like we were meant to be together. I know that you are that special someone that God made only for me and I just don't want to lose you baby." Tinka said as she looked up at me and I knew that everything she said was true.

That made me forget all about the picture and wanting to have a talk, so much so that I couldn't even say a word. I just leaned down and kissed Tinka passionately, darting my tongue inside of her mouth and massaging hers with mine. That was enough to arouse her like I was and before I knew it she had sat up and slipped her peach colored gown over her head.

"I want you Quatty. Right now," Tinka panted as I quickly stood up and pulled her up to her feet.

She just didn't know how much I wanted her but after I stripped down, asshole naked in a matter of seconds, I think she got the point.

"I want you too baby. I do. No, I need you Nicole. I love you girl." I said as I stepped closer to her and lifted her up into my arms.

Before I knew it Tinka had wrapped her legs around my waist as I kissed and carried her into the bedroom. Once inside I laid her in the King-sized bed and stood over her as she panted and rubbed her erect nipples.

"Ohhh Quatty come here." Tinka said as she bit her bottom lip and I massaged my massive dick while I looked down at her.

She was perfect in every way, all beautiful, bronze and glowing. I wanted to just stand there and admire the Goddess I called my own but my manhood wanted no parts of waiting. He throbbed every time I skimmed Tinka's body sending an intense tingle down my spine. After standing there a few seconds and feeling my dick grow harder and harder by the second, I just couldn't take it anymore so I dived in Tinka's wetness and damn near got lost at sea. As soon as I penetrated her I felt like I fell into the softest, wettest cotton ball on earth as she scratched my back, moaned my name, and squeezed her walls around my dick. I dug deeper inside of her as I looked into her eyes and hoped that what she had to tell me wouldn't end what we had.

"Damn baby I love you. I mean that Nicole, just don't take my love for granted. Please baby." I whispered into Tinka's ear as I battered her g-spot and licked that delicate patch of skin behind her ear.

I felt her get wetter and wetter with each lick as she continued to grip her walls, grind her hips, and fuck me back from the bottom. She fucked me like a pro, so much so I didn't even anticipate her next move. For a second I was like the bitch as I got caught up in the swirl motion Tinka was doing with her hips until she suddenly flipped me over and got on top. Before I could protest or even think she was sticking my manhood back inside her wetness and riding me into ecstasy. I had to grab her hips and hold on as she swirled, and twerked on my stick like a stripper. I sat up and held her close to me as I took one of her breast in my mouth and tried to hold back my nut which was about to explode.

"Ahhh shit baby. I'm gonna bust baby." I yelled out as Tinka yelled that she was too and we thrust our bodies together faster and harder than before.

After a few seconds of that the nut I chased, like a crackhead chases a rock, hit me hard. Shakes took over my body as Tinka wrapped her arms around my neck and grinded us both into euphoria.

"Yesssss daddy. YEESSSSSSS!" Tinka yelled as we both came together, moaning and kissing until our shakes stopped.

When it was over I fell back on to the bed and Tinka fell on top of me breathing hard and moaning.

"I love you girl, no matter what!" I said to Tinka before I closed my eyes and sleep slowly took over my body.

"Just don't break my heart." I mumbled through my sleepy haze before my thoughts and fatigue whisked me away.

# Chapter 2

The sound of Tinka throwing her fucking guts up awoke me the next morning and I quickly jumped out of bed and ran to the bathroom to check on her.

"Tinka baby, you alright?" I asked like the stupid ass people in the movies, knowing damn well she wasn't okay because she was puking her guts out.

I could tell that was her thoughts too as she turned slightly and gave me a, nigga really look before she proceeded to vomit. I took that as my cue to shut the fuck up and just be a supportive boyfriend and baby daddy so I grabbed her 28 inch bundles in my hand and held it up out of the vomit while I rubbed her back with the other hand.

"Damn baby, it's gonna be okay. Lil man got you sick as hell. I'm already ready for this to be over so you can be comfortable again. The last thing I want to do is be the cause of yo pain." I said speaking more so on the drama than the baby as Tinka blew her last chunk, wiped her mouth on a piece of tissue, and slowly stood up.

I helped her to her feet before I quickly dashed out of the bathroom to get bleach, fabuloso, the mop, and some paper towels. I was back in a flash and began to clean up the mess my baby had made as she washed her face and brushed her teeth. I glanced over at her once I was done cleaning and caught her gazing at me through the mirror and the look on her face made my fucking heart skip a beat. I knew that look meant that Tinka was ready to have that talk from the night before but something inside of me told me that what she was going to say was something I didn't want to hear.

That's why I quickly looked away from her and left the room to return the cleaning supplies to the pantry. I took my time getting back to the bathroom from the kitchen as my mind roamed and heart raced in my chest. When I walked back into the bathroom Tinka was still standing in the same spot at the sink as tears ran down her face. I walked up beside her and wiped them away as I looked into her eyes and they told me everything I needed to know. I knew what she was about to say would change everything and that made me nervous. I had to turn away and grab my toothbrush to try and ignore the fear I had inside.

"Quatty baby, I think I should tell you what I have to say right now." Tinka said to me as I cut on my electric toothbrush and pretended that the gentle hum of the motor was preventing me from hearing her.

Doing that, I was able to buy a little time because Tinka didn't start back talking until my petty ass had finished brushing, flossed, and rinsed my mouth out twice. I was trying anything I could do to avoid that shit, even though the night before I had wanted it so badly. Time to think had made me see that some shit wasn't meant for us to know because the truth hurt way more than ignorance. I wished my black ass would have never pressed the issue or even opened that damn box as soon as Tinka started talking.

"Quatty, I really don't know if there is an easy way to say what I'm about to say so I'm just going to say it. Before I say anything though I just have to say again that I love you." Tinka said as she turned to look at me and I shifted from foot to foot.

I felt fidgety as fuck, like a kid waiting in the principal's office as I stood there and watched tears fall from her eyes. I couldn't imagine the shit she was about to say that had her so torn but I knew I wouldn't like it. That didn't stop her from telling me though.

"You know I love you, don't you Quatty?" Tinka asked as I shook my head yes and sat on the counter next to the sink.

For some reason, I felt like I needed to brace myself for what she was about to say and having my ass on marble was just what I needed. I sat there with my hands folded in front of me and stared at the woman I loved as she walked closer and grabbed my hand like I was the girl and she was the man in the relationship, and she was telling me she had an affair. My heart raced like a bitch too as I sat there and watched tear after tear fall from her eyes, but felt no sympathy. I couldn't feel her pain when I was in pain of my own. I had turned that soft side of me off again as I stared at her with an ice stare and waited on her to speak again.

"Quatty, what I'm about to say may change the way you view our relationship but I want you to know that my love for you has always been true." Tinka said as her words made my heart twitch and I gently jerked my hand back.

I don't know why I did that, but something inside of me told me that I didn't want to be touching Tinka when she finally gave me her news. Matter of fact something told me I didn't even want to see her beautiful ass so I closed my eyes as I felt her reach for my hand again and I quickly moved away.

"Quatty please don't be like that baby. I love you and that's why I'm saying this… We didn't meet by chance. It was all a part of HIS plan." Tinka said as my fucking eyes instantly snapped open and I glared into her face.

"A part of who's mutha fucking plan Tinka? Huh? What the fuck going on?" I yelled as I watched her eyes grow in fear but I really didn't give a fuck.

I quickly stood up and towered over Tinka, looking down on her sad and nervous face as anxiety and rage brewed inside of me. I couldn't believe that beautiful bitch. I had sacrificed my life and freedom for her, for us and she would prepay me by telling me some nigga had put her on me in the first place. That shit broke my heart into a million pieces and seriously made me question whether or not she was worth all I had gone through. I sucked in a deep breath and put my fists up to my temples as I tried to calm the anger inside of me. I had to pace back and forth in front of the sink for a minute to count and try to calm down. I knew if I didn't I would say something I would regret, and despite the hurt and ager I felt, I didn't want to lose Tinka. I just wanted her to be fucking honest with me like I had been honest with her. Not try to touch and hold me while she cried, like she was doing.

"Nah Maine Tinka. Hold up." I said as I grabbed her arms and gently pushed her back.

"Tell me what's going on first." I said as I folded my arms in front of me and leaned against the counter.

I stood there for a few seconds as I waited on her to finish crying long enough to talk and just thought about whether or not I would walk away if she said the wrong shit. I didn't know what I would do when that time came, but when she opened her mouth again I knew I was going to find out.

"This all started about a month before we met and my ex, Dip, contacted me from jail. He knew my sister's address from years before so he wrote this sorrowful apology letter, begging me to come see him. Like a fool bent on facing the demon who haunted my dreams and conquering him, I went down there to visit him. During our visit, everything was going good with me doing most of the talking and him just sitting there. He let me get everything off of my chest then he cried like I had never seen him cry before. And just like he planned, he had me then and he didn't let up. He acted like that dude I met back in the day, all humble and loving and shit. I fed right into that bullshit and let my guard down. Hell, I even took a picture with him." Tinka said as I continued to stand there and glare at her while I clenched my jaws together.

I was about to fucking explode hearing all of that shit so late into the game. Shit I never even expected. After all of the horrible shit she had told me that nigga did to her, I never thought she would ever want to think about him again, let alone take a fucking picture. Besides, we had been together almost six months and had been through hell and back together. We lost a fucking child and was blessed with another one, yet she still kept shit from me. That shit didn't sit well with me and I couldn't hide my hurt and anger as I pushed Tinka back again when she tried to hug me.

"Quatty please baby just let me finish but don't push me away. I took a friend like picture with him that day, and he admitted to all of his wrongs something he had never done." Tinka said as she tried to grab my arms and I pushed her hands away.

I felt tears begin to well up in my eyes and I pushed her back again and quickly grinded the tears away with my fists before I nodded my head and told her to proceed.

"That's what drew me in. That's what clouded my judgement and left me vulnerable to his manipulation." Tinka said as she cried and I sucked my teeth.

"Almost towards the end of the visit he flipped shit on me though when I told him that I could never fuck with him again. See, I only went to see him for closure, not reconciliation. That's not what he wanted though so he did what he did best. He threatened to take away the one thing he knew I had in the world and that was my sister and her kids if I didn't do him one favor for snitching and sending him to jail. Knowing the nigga he was and what he was capable of I had no choice but to sit there and at least listen to what he wanted me to do while I thought of a way out."

"When he said that he just needed me to go to the club and party on him, then find his lil young homeboy he was throwing a surprise party for to chill for the night, I thought about it. He wanted me to have fun with him, then take him to this surprise house party he was setting up at a spot out in Millington. It sounded all innocent and shit to me right then, so I instantly got on alert knowing Dip's grimy ass. I told him I would think about it before I left, but something inside of me told me what he was asking me to do was deeper than he said. After I got home and called my sister and told her what Dip wanted she confirmed my suspicion. She made me see that I was being made to be a set up bitch and that Dip was going to kill whoever the nigga was I had to bring to him. With that knowledge, I decided I wasn't going to do it so I ignored his calls and every letter he sent to my sister's house I had her burn. About a week after that shit got real though when someone tried to run my sister off the road with her kids in the car. I got a call from the police that day followed by one from Dip telling me that was just a warning. He told me to be ready and on call to go get this man and bring him to him. Weeks passed after that and I was on edge every minute. Dip sent daily reminders both threatening and nonthreatening to keep my mind on track too. Then one day he called me and said that I had to be at Club Empire in an hour. He told me the man was named Quaderious Jones, but everybody called him Quatty and I could find you in VIP." Tinka said and all the air left my body, but I held my shit together.

I just stood there and bit my bottom lip while I nodded my head telling her to go on.

"So, you see me meeting you at the bar that night was not by chance. I had searched the club for hours looking for you. When I did find you though, I fell in love instantly, but not enough to let my family die. So yeah, for a few hours I played the game and got close to you. The only thing was the more I tried to pretend to like you, the more I actually did. By the time you were helping me to the car after the gunfire I had fell off the cliff, and was lost in a sea of your love. I wanted out of everything at that moment, which is why I had you go to my house that night and not where he told me to bring you. I called and had my sister go into hiding with the kids once we were back at my place and I went to the bathroom. I sent a text to his phone too and told him I was out and if he did anything I would give his seeds the same fate he promised my family. By the time Pooh called the next morning I was on edge, scared of what Dip would do. At that time, I had no idea why he wanted you or that Dip knew Pooh at all. She revealed that shit in the first half of our phone call though, telling me that I had fucked up." Tinka said as I bucked my eyes at her.

I couldn't believe that shit.

"So later that day after your car got fucked off I called my cousins and had them do what they do best. They got me a little insurance policy on Dip in the form of pics of his kids at school and I called and played the same game he did. I sent him a picture from my phone of his twin girls and told him if the shit didn't stop and he didn't control Pooh, his little babies were dead. I think that made my point clear to him because he knew my cousins but it did nothing for Pooh. She got on the phone cursing and ranting as usual and I told her if she didn't leave you alone her kids would meet the same fate. I didn't want to say that shit because the last thing I would ever do is hurt a child, but I had no choice. I had to do something to protect you. To protect us. All of us."

"So, it was Pooh you saw me on the phone with when I walked up. After that I lost all contact with Dip and Pooh, other than her usual harassment. I didn't care about his threats after that because I knew there wasn't anything we couldn't defeat together. I loved you from the start baby and that's the truth Quatty. I'm so sorry baby. Please forgive me. I know I should have told you all of this that night, but I thought I had it all under control. I thought I could end it and shit wouldn't have gotten out of hand. We lost our baby because of me, because I wished ill will on other people's kids and I will never forgive myself for that. I'll never forgive myself for lying to you either, but I hope someday you will. Will you Quatty? Will you please forgive me? I love you Quatty." Tinka said as she wrapped her arms around my neck and the tears I had held back streamed down my face.

Everything I knew was a lie because the woman I loved and thought had saved me had betrayed my trust. I didn't know if there was any coming back from that, but when I looked down into her tear-filled, beautiful eyes I knew I could forgive her someday. I just didn't know when.

"If you can't even forgive yourself, how the fuck can you ask me to forgive you? Huh?" I asked her through clenched teeth as I bent down and pressed my forehead to hers.

My body trembled as I breathed like a dragon and struggled to contain my rage.

"You betrayed me Tinka. You! Just let me go maine. I gotta get the fuck out of here." I said as I peeled her arms from around my neck and pushed her to the side.

As soon as she was safely out of the way I stormed out of the bathroom and straight to the front door as she cried and ran behind me.

"Please Quatty wait. Please baby, we can work through this. I love you Quatty, please. I love you. Don't you love me?" Tinka screamed when I stopped to open the door before I calmly turned and looked at her.

"Yes, I love you and I always will, but I don't know if I can forgive you." I said flatly, void of feelings at the moment, numb but full of pain.

I turned back around and snatched open the door as she grabbed the back of my shirt and I tried to wiggle free. As soon as I was free of her grip and opened the screen door to step out on the porch, I felt a force hit me from the side and the wind leave my body. The next thing I knew I was on the ground and I had a dozen knees and boots in my back and neck.

Two Memphis Police Officers who both had their knees in my back told me I was being detained on suspicion of murder, attempted murder, and two counts of aggravated assault before they read me my rights, and dragged my black ass to the car. I let them bitches drag me too, I didn't even try to put up a fight. I didn't give a fuck at that moment so I couldn't even care that they were punching and jerking my ass all around.

All I could do was stare at Tinka, the beautiful, seductive temptress who betrayed my trust. I watched her as she screamed from the porch and called my name, begging me to forgive her. Tears rolled down my face as I bit my bottom lip and shook my head at her with the thought of telling her that I probably never could. I couldn't say shit, just stare as tears blurred my vision and my heart ached.

I kept my eyes on her until the cop jumped into the car and we pulled away from the curb. When she was out of my view I just closed my eyes and let my head rest on the back of the seat. There I was again, in police custody wondering where the fuck I had gone wrong. I couldn't help but to wonder would my trust of a bitch ultimately be my demise. I thought about that shit all the way down to 201 and to the fourth floor, homicide division. Detective Lundy met us at the door and quickly led me to an interrogation room.

As soon as we were inside he started the bullshit, offering me a cigarette and something to eat. Even though I knew that bullshit First 48 tactics well, I still took his shit and sat there silently until he came back with it. He didn't know it, but the only thing that I was prepared to say was that I wanted a lawyer. I just wanted to fuck with his bitch ass and eat my last meal before he sent me back into the belly of the beast.

When he came back with my $5 fill up from KFC, a pack of Newport's, and a 2-liter Peach Nehi, I quickly took his shit and began to eat. I barely even heard all the trap a nigga questions he asked as I munched and thought about how Tinka had betrayed me. When I finally finished eating I lit a Newport and sat back in my chair to look the detective in the face. I hit the cigarette hard and long, sucking up half of it in one puff as I stared his ass down.

"So, Mr. Jones are you ready to tell me where you were last night? I have reason to believe you were involved in a homicide on the east side of the city so I need your side of the story to clear things up. The sooner you talk to me and stop bullshitting the sooner you can get out of here. Now, what's it gonna be? Are you gonna cooperate and tell me all that you know and possibly return to your life? Or are you gonna keep sitting here like a dumb ass and let me lock yo ass up and throw away the key? The choice is yours." Detective Lundy said as he smirked and then sat forward in his chair to whisper to me.

"I tell you what though, ain't a muthafucking school or medical practice in this world gonna take yo ass after a murder charge so you better choose wisely." Lundy said as his green eyes flickered with satisfaction and he smirked again while I put my hand on my head.

I made his bitch ass think I was stressing or possibly thinking of a story or some shit as I sat with my hands on my head and deeply exhaled. I could hear the excitement in his bitch ass as he cleared his throat and I kept my head down and pretended like he had my ass ready to confess that quickly. He had me fucked up though because the last thing I was going to do was open my fucking mouth and incriminate myself. Instead I sat there for a while with my head down, one hand on my head and the other up to my mouth as I lit another Newport to puff on. I heard him snicker like he had accomplished some shit a few minutes later and I decided it was time to end his little interrogation. I suddenly and slowly sat back up in my chair and stared at him in his eyes as he shook his head and tried to coax me to talk.

"Come on Quaderious, I looked at your record so I know you're a good guy. I know you were on the right path and you may have just gotten caught up, but I can help you out of this. Tell me what happened Quaderious." Detective Lundy asked as I stared him down and pretended to be struggling to find the words to say.

I played his bitch ass like he was about to get a confession, had him on the edge of his fucking seat and just when he put his pen to the snitch paper he was compiling, I burst his fucking bubble. My cold, eerie laugh quickly filled the room and Lundy looked up at me in disbelief.

"Oh, you know me huh? Well, if you know me so FUCKING well you know I want a lawyer and if you ain't charging me you bitches can let me the fuck go. You know that huh?" I said as I hit my cigarette again and blew the smoke out right in his bitch ass face before I began to laugh again.

That pissed him off so bad his little pink ass instantly turned beet red and jumped up and stormed out of the room. I made sure that my laugh followed him out of the door and didn't stop laughing as I looked up at the camera I was sure was there and threw up a middle finger sign.

"Fuck 12 nigga, let me the fuck go." I yelled out before I put my cigarette out on the table and sat back in the chair, ready to wait their asses out.

I knew them bitches couldn't hold me but 72 hours without charging me so I just hoped that Pooh wouldn't say shit before then. I was just gonna sit there silent and try to figure out how I could get over what Tinka had done. I sat there for hours with her voice ringing in my ears and the vision of her face in my mind. Part of me wanted to be done with her ole deceitful ass, but another part of me just wouldn't let go. I thought about my baby and all Tinka and I had been through in our short time together and I felt like that was too much to let slip away. Besides, we had a baby growing inside of her that didn't ask to come into the world. That's why I felt like I had to at least try to get past what Tinka did, but I knew that shit wouldn't be easy.

Every time I looked at her I would think about how she was about to lead me to my death, but then that voice in my head would say, "But she didn't". That voice was right, she hadn't done it. Instead she risked everything she knew and loved to be with me. That was the fact that brought me back to reality and helped to soften my heart. By the time a plain clothed cop came to get me and take me over to a holding cell, I had made up my mind to forgive Tinka once I made her understand how much she had hurt me.

I felt lighter as I walked into the dirty, cramped cell that held 12 other niggas and quickly took a seat on the bench by the bars. I knew them bitches were going to employ their right to hold me for that 72 while they tried to find someone to finger me so I didn't even sweat it. I just laughed at the little short, fat, white, dough boy looking ass police boy as he told me to get comfortable.

"Pussy, I'm always comfortable. Unlike bitches like you, real niggas don't fold. Now, go tell Detective Lundy bitch ass to hurry up and get this witch hunt over with and get back here to let me the fuck out. Y'all bitches ain't got shit on me, so let me the fuck go." I said as other niggas in the cell cheered and joined in on the fun.

The police boy looked like he had shit his pants as he quickly scurried away from the bars and fumbled with the keys as he opened the door.

"And I want my phone call muthafucka. You bitches can't make my black ass sit in here without a phone call. I know my muthafucking rights!" I yelled as he turned and said okay before he disappeared through the door.

I laughed as the scared shitless expression on his face flashed in my mind and I wondered had he really shit his pants.

"You da real deal beast that nigga lil homie. That's wasup my guy. Wasup witcha though?" Some tall, bald head nigga with golds who was sitting beside me asked as I mean mugged him.

I wasn't with that friendly shit especially not in my current state of mind so I quickly made that shit known.

"Look my nigga, this shit ain't summer camp and I ain't looking for no mutha fucking best friend. It's 7-4 till the world blow with me all day. So, what yo G like?" I asked that nigga as I stood up eye to eye with his big ass and threw up the pitch folk.

He returned love and I softened a little when I found out him and most of the niggas in the cell were my brothers. After that I sat there and kicked shit with them niggas until a C.O. brought around those hard, rotten ass bologna sandwiches and I asked about my phone call. Lucky for me the guard was a bitch, something short and thick with red hair named Lilly. I quickly turned on my school boy, pretty nigga charm and got her to go see about my call. That lil bitch must have had a little pull with the watch commander too because twenty minutes later she was coming back and taking me out to the phone.

I told her how fine she was as she dialed the number for me and put the phone to my ear. I made my chin graze her hand when I positioned the phone, and when she didn't jerk back I knew I had her. She was going to be my go to bitch, as my cousin Big Moe called them. That's the inside bitch I could get to do all my dirt. I could tell it was in her too when she giggled and winked her eye before she stepped back to let me make my call. I gave that bitch a pimp wink and then waited for my mama to answer so that I could tell her what had happened.

I asked her not to do anything to get me out as she cried into the phone because it was my mess and I had to clean it up on my own. She promised that she wouldn't and told me Tinka had been calling before I asked her to call her on three-way. I told her to mute the phone when she clicked back over and on the second ring Tinka answered. Her voice was so sad and worried I almost said something, but I just listened instead. I loved that damn girl so much, but I had to make her suffer for a while. After Tinka said hello ten times and I didn't say anything my mama got the picture and quickly hung up. When she did I told her what had happened and she gave me some motherly advice.

"Forgive her Quatty. You have to because I know you love her and she loves you. Everyone makes mistakes baby, but it's what you do after the wrong that counts. She told you Quaderious that's all that matters so think about your baby. That child didn't ask to be born into a bad situation so you gotta do all you can to make it right. When you get out this time I want you gone, away from Memphis and all this mess. I want you to live my son, and live well. Here you will never be able to do that. This is our last time here son. Please." My mama pleaded as she cried into the phone and my heart broke.

I hated to hear my mama cry, especially when I knew I was the cause of her pain. I knew she was right anyway, I had to forgive Tinka because I had done my share of shit too.

"I will mama. I promise." I told her right before the automated service told me that I had sixty seconds left on the call.

I quickly told my mama I loved her and to tell Tinka I loved her too before we hung up the phone. I felt all sentimental and shit when I got off the phone with my mama and I had to shake that shit off before I turned back around to the lil thick C.O. I didn't want to fuck up and make the bitch think I was weak because that would fuck up my chances. That's why I dug deep inside and pulled my ice grill back up and turned back around to face her with my mug on. That lil undercover freaky hoe smiled instantly and licked her lips letting me know that she was the type of bitch I never probably shouldn't fuck with on the outside, but could use as long as I was locked up.

I couldn't help it but I thought of her as one of them going ass bitches who craved power because she was weak ass hell in real life. I figured that's why the bitch had become a C.O. in the first place; so she could finally be in charge and quench her thirst for unlimited dick at the same time. She had me fucked up though because I had no intentions of ever letting that hoe taste daddy dick, but I would tease her with the thought. Despite all that was going on, Tinka was the only chick I wanted but I knew behind bars I had to do what I had to do. That's why I turned that Quatty charm on and flashed that bitch a sneaky seductive smile before I bit my bottom lip and winked my eye at her.

I could damn near see that bitch's panties get wet right then as she brushed up on me and then told me to follow her. I will admit I watched her fat ass as she led me back to my cell, but I still didn't want to be the three thousandth nigga to get inside of her. Hell, naw that wasn't me. I played the roll though and told her thanks with her sexy ass before she smiled and locked me back in. She kept her eyes on me as she backed to the door and when she got there I blew her a kiss. That was the nail in that bitch's coffin because she cheesed so damn hard she couldn't even get the key card in the door. I held back my laughter until she was finally out the pod then me and the homies let loose.

"You got you one, didn't you bruh." Turk the big nigga who I had first met in the holding cell said as I went back to my bench to sit down.

"Hell naw, I don't want that hoe. I got a good woman waiting on me. I am gonna use that bitch though cause I got a feeling I'm gonna be here a minute." I said to him as he nodded and I sat back to think.

After three more hours passed I knew I was right, I wasn't going any fucking where. Later when a C.O. came and took us to processing and started assigning us to four man cells in the processing pod, I knew them bitches had found something to hold me on. I didn't sweat it though I just went my ass in my cell and laid it down, ready to do my time. The next day the police came and told me they had a witness that placed me on the scene so I was officially being charged.

Them saying they had a witness gave me hope because I knew that witness wasn't Pooh. I knew if it was her there would have been more charges added cause she evil as fuck like that. That's why I still felt unfazed as I went about my day, ready to get on the floor with my cuzzo. Two days after that I got a visit from the one person I really wanted to see. I walked into the visitation room with the intention of making her ass suffer and beg but as soon as I saw Tinka's flawless caramel face and brown slanted eyes I fell in love all over again and there was no way that I could stay mad.

I damn near ran over to the table as soon as the cuffs were off me and I was cleared to move. As soon as I got to the table I swallowed my pride and wrapped Tinka up in my arms to give her a kiss. Our kiss with tears all over both of our faces, was the most passionate, loving kiss I had ever felt. We said all that had to be said with our tongues, hearts, and eyes in that instant and I felt like I never wanted to let her go. I had to though because the next thing I knew the C.O. was yelling for us to separate. I quickly kissed my baby hand and rubbed her belly telling my baby I loved him before I helped Tinka into the chair and then sat down myself.

"Baby let me start by saying I'm sorry. I never meant to hurt you Quatty and I will never forgive myself for deceiving you. I promise I will never keep anything from you again my King. I promise." Tinka said as tears ran down her cheeks and I reached over to wipe them away.

I never realized how soft her skin was until that moment but it felt like silk under my fingers. Her beautiful, teary eyes were like stars too, shining brightly on me and lifting my spirits. There was no way I could be angry at her after seeing her face and seeing how much her actions were hurting her too. I didn't want her carrying around that guilt though so I did my best to ease her mind.

"Baby don't apologize anymore, you did enough of that already. I understand. I understand why you had to do it and I also understand why you didn't go through with it. You love me and I love you and ain't no changing that no matter what. So, you dry those beautiful eyes and let me see that smile I fell in love with." I told Tinka as I wiped her tears away once again and she smiled big and bright.

The rest of my visit with her went smoothly with her telling me that she invited her sister and kids to come down and stay with her for a while. I was happy to hear that too because the last thing I wanted was for her to be alone with Pooh and Lay Lay still on the loose. She told me she went down and got a restraining order on them both too, to cover herself when she killed them. I had to laugh when she said that because she sounded like a real gangsta sitting there with a fat belly and shit. After that she told me she had gotten me a lawyer and that he would be to see me the next day.

"His name is Langston Rogers and he is the best criminal defense lawyer in Memphis that money can buy. I have to get you out of here my king, by any means necessary." Tinka said as I think I began to love her even more.

That girl was my backbone for real and I was lucky to have her. We chatted the rest of the visit and when it was time to go I didn't want to release my grip on her. I told her we were getting married when I got out and my baby left with a huge smile on her face. Hell, I had one too. I floated back to the fucking cell and laid down early with Tinka on my mind.

The next morning, I was up early, anxious to meet my lawyer and see what he had to say. Right after breakfast I got called down and was led to the lawyer conference room by Lilly, the thick C.O. I didn't even really flirt with the bitch that time because my mind was too preoccupied with Tinka and my case. I did give her a little wink and air kiss though after she un-cuffed me and I stepped into the room. That was enough to keep that bitch on the string and make her giggle her ass off all the way out of the room.

I watched her until she was out of view then I sat down in front of the young, black, hood looking lawyer dressed in slacks and a blue polo shirt. I quickly skimmed that nigga from head to toe and then caught a glimpse of the star of David on his neck, right behind his right ear.

"PML brother." I said as he quickly looked up from the papers he was rummaging through and gave me a smirk that let me know it was love.

"Nothing but love bruh. Aye, I can't talk like that in here because this shit be recorded but it's nothing but love folk." My lawyer whispered before he quickly sat back, straight in his chair.

"Well hello Mr. Jones, I am attorney Langston Rogers but you can call me L. Now, your fiancée Nicole contacted me to represent you so that's what I'm here to do. Before we proceed I have to ask you." L said as he leaned forward and began to whisper again.

"Did you do it." he whispered before he sat back in his chair and stared at me.

I gave that nigga a, what the fuck you think look, before I shook my head no and he sat back up straight in his seat. He knew exactly what the fuck that meant and the look on his face told me he already knew it anyway.

"So Mr. Jones, did you commit the crimes you are being accused of?" he asked again before he winked his eye.

"No!" I said and he shook his head before he began to take out papers from his brief case.

"That's just what I thought. Your fiancée filled me in on all that has happened and told me that this is all a part of the harassment you all have encountered from your ex Mariah. Now Mariah is still in the hospital in critical condition and police are waiting for her statement to officially charge you with a number of additional charges. I've already filed motions this morning to get the charges dropped due to lack of evidence or get your bail reduced. Right now, they have you on $250,000 bond. That's just a formality so I'm going to work my end and get that lowered. Now, I just need you to keep a leveled head and let me do my job. Do you have any questions for me?" L asked and I shook my head no.

I didn't have any questions because I knew he had me, he was my brother so he had no choice. I felt confident shit would work in my favor so the only thing I really wanted to know was my release date. It must have been apparent on my face too because the next thing I knew he had leaned in again to whisper.

"You need to talk to the bitch and tell her to keep her fucking mouth closed." L said before he quickly sat back and began to pack up his shit.

I felt him on that because that had been on my mind since he said they were waiting on her statement. I thanked him for all he was doing after I watched him pack his shit then the C.O. came back to get me. When I got back to my cell I felt like I had a mission, one that could alter my life. For a week I called different people, trying to get word to Pooh. Some of the people I called said they would tell her, some pretended not to know me, and some hung up the fucking phone in my face. I didn't let that get to me though, I just kept trying until I called her cousin Pam and she told me she was out of the hospital.

I asked her to pass the word and she told me that she would. I felt scared as fuck for the first time after that call because dealing with Pooh you could never tell what would happen. The day after the call I found out what I feared most and that was that she had made a statement. They came to get me a little after midnight with the riot squad in tow to take me back to the Penial Farm to await trial. I don't know why they thought I was going to act a fool or cause an uproar but they had me fucked up. I was too numb at that point to do anything but walk my black ass out and get on that bus. I found a seat near the back and quickly sat down as my heart broke once again.

"Damn fucked off again because of the same bitch. Ain't no bitch worth this. But in the end, that hoe gonna pay." I said to myself as I leaned my head against the cage metal screen on the window and got my last glimpse at freedom for a while.

# Chapter 3

When the bus pulled up in front of the Penial Farm I got a bitter sweet feeling inside. It was fucked up but a small part of me felt like I was at home again. At least behind those walls I knew exactly what to expect and I didn't have to worry about the cops coming to snatch my ass up because I was already there. That's what I told myself to calm the anxiety inside as I filed off the bus and in line to go inside just like all of the other inmates. I walked inside in a daze and stood in the hall like a zombie, numb as fuck while I went through the same intake process I had been through months before. Familiar faces of guards and inmates alike flashed before my eyes but I remained stoic the entire time. I didn't even react to C.O. Wallace as he welcomed me back to hell.

"I knew you'd be back you little bitch. Well, welcome to your new hell. I'm gonna make your life a fucking nightmare boy." The big, black, bitch whispered in my ear as I finished dressing out but I didn't even flinch.

I had made it up in my mind I'd get him, but I'd be quiet about all of my movements that time around. I knew the police were looking for any reason they could find to throw my black, almost militant ass into the deepest darkest hole they could find and I was not about to give them a reason to. That's why I buried my thoughts of breaking his fucking face as he led me back to F Pod with my cousin and all the brothers I had left behind. It was like a damn convict reunion as soon as I walked in and everybody saw my face.

"BROTHER ON THE FLOOR. THAT NIGGA QUATTY BACK!" one brother yelled from the top tier as he banged on the bars with his fists.

"QUATTY! MY NIGGA BACK. BIG MOE…QUATTY BACK BIG BRUH!" my lil homie Lil Click yelled as he quickly ran over to open Moe's door before he dashed over to me.

He had a fucking kool-aid smile on his face as he shook up with me quickly then grabbed my mat and shit out of my hand.

"Damn bruh, I ain't gonna say I'm happy to see you in a fucked up place like this. But it damn shole feel good to have you back. Shit crazy in here big bruh." Lil Click said as he led me back to the cell I had shared with Moe while other brothers showed me love along the way.

Niggas handed me soups, snacks, and joints after they shook me up and by the time I made it to the door and Big Moe who was waiting, I had a damn grocery store in my arms.

"Damn lil cuz, you back again?" Moe said to me with a happy but pained expression on his face as Lil Click pushed pass him into the cell to sit my shit down.

Big Moe continued to look at me like nigga why you here, as he grabbed some of the shit out of my arms. I tried to hide the shameful look I was sure was on my face as I shook my head to say that I didn't know why I was back and walked into the cell behind Moe.

"Yeah big cuz, that bitch caught me up again. I had to body the nigga too. That hoe tried to get me on that set up shit. The nigga jumped out on my ass." I said to Big Moe as he sat down on his plush ass bunk by the window and I went back to the one he had reserved for me.

It was like even though he didn't want me to, he knew I would be back so he kept my shit just like it was. I was happy he had too as I sat down on my soft ass mattress and propped up against the wall. I watched as Moe and Lil Click riffled through the gifts everybody had given me and take out the things they wanted while my mind tried to get used to being confined again. I sat there and just stared into space as I tried to think of how I would change shit when I got out so that I wouldn't end up in that bitch again. I must have gotten deep into thought because I didn't even hear Moe calling my name until he threw a pack of noodles across the room and hit me in the head.

"Damn lil nigga. I been sitting here calling you for a minute and you didn't hear shit. That bitch really got yo mind huh?" Big Moe asked as he snickered a little while biting into the Snicker he had taken out of my shit.

I sighed as I rubbed my hand across my waves and shook my head because I knew he was right. That bitch did have my mind fucked up and that was something I just couldn't hide.

"Yeah, I'm fucked up big homie. So much shit went down out there. I don't know if I can ever bounce back from this though." I said as I shook my head and Moe's expression changed from amused to serious.

I watched as wrinkles formed in his forehead and that twinkle that only came into his eyes when he had a plan appeared.

"Yeah lil cuzz, I know. You know my fucking ears stay to the street so I already know what went down with the Pooh bitch and that nigga Big Dip. I also know that nigga supposedly got hittas in here that supposed to be waiting on you to hit the floor. I know all that shit and I also know ain't shit finna shake up in here. You know the brothers got yo back and I got a hit on any nigga head in here who feel tough enough to step to you. All you gotta do is watch yo back and stay ready to keep from having to get ready." Big Moe said as he quickly pulled a butch from under his pillow and motioned for me to come get it.

I got up quickly and took the short, sharp piece of metal with a homemade handle into my hand and stuck it into my underwear.

"Keep that butch on you at all times lil nigga. 12 ain't gonna fuck with you about it because they on my payroll so you ain't gotta worry about that. Now that we got that straight I can help you out on the other binds you in too. I got a sure fire way for you to bounce back while you locked up, so you will guarantee you straight when you hit the streets again." Moe said as he reached his hand under the same pillow he had pulled the butch from under and flashed me a bag of a white, crystal like substance.

I couldn't tell what it was right off because I wasn't into the dope game like that. What I did know was that I really wanted no parts of the dope game with so much shit already hanging over my head. Deep in my heart I still had hope that one day soon all of my troubles would disappear and I'd be able to return to my internship and my quest to become a doctor. That was the foolish hope I held onto and as I looked at the for sure death sentence Moe held in his hand and I shook my head no, I wasn't ready to let that hope go.

"Nah big homie, I'm straight on that shit. For now anyway. I gotta see how this shit go before I jump into that water again." I said to Moe as he shook his head that he understood and returned his stash to his spot.

He told me that he respected my decision but he would be willing to put me down if I ever became ready. I told him I would definitely take him up on that offer if shit went wrong. After that me, him, and lil Click sat around the cell and ate snacks as they told me everything that had been going on. They told me how the Vice Lords, a rival gang, were trying to take over the drug trade inside the jail and had gotten one of their officers on payroll flapped.

"Yeah them bitches looking for a slick war behind that. They took out one of my top C.O.'s. She was the bitch bringing in over $10,000 worth of dope a week. I don't think we'll find another hoe like her. Durty been looking though. That's the heaviest nigga in here who happens to be my lil homie from back in the day. Me and that nigga been moving hella product the last few years. He get the dope for the low and I get it in, that's our system. I just gotta find a new way to uphold my end of the deal while mercking the competition." Big Moe said as he shook his head and stared out into the pod with a serious expression on his face.

I could see his mind moving as he skimmed the two female guards who were entering our pod on new assignment. I could tell he was sizing them up and seeing which one would be easy to manipulate. He didn't even have to do that though when I realized one of the girls was Lilly, my lil thick junt from the processing pod.

"Aye bruh, I definitely can help with that." I said as I noticed Lilly smiling at me and quickly blew her a small kiss.

Her eyes lit up instantly after that, as she skipped off behind the commanding officer to find out which pods she would secure.

"Oh, I saw that shit." Lil Click said as he watched Lilly watch me until she disappeared into the security door with the rest of the officers.

"Yeah I saw that shit too. What the fuck was that about ole pussy whipped ass nigga?" Big Moe asked as he and Lil Click laughed and I gave them the rundown on me and Lilly.

By the time I finished talking Big Moe and Lil Click were excited as fuck because they knew just like I did, that Lilly was the bitch we needed.

"Maine, I know you said you don't wonna jump off the porch just yet lil cuzz but as soon as you know something we need to jump on this. We got enough dope in reserve for about a month but before then I need you to make a decision." Big Moe said as I shook my head that I understood.

"In the meantime though, keep buttering that lil bitch up. I know you love yo wife and all but behind these walls lil cuz, don't none of that shit apply. A prison hoe to move yo work ain't got nothing to do with the love you have for your woman on the outside lil bruh. Remember that. Behind these walls, we are who we have to be and never forget that." Big Moe said as I agreed and Lil Click chimed in.

We sat there and chopped it up about hoes, life, and getting money until Lilly came around with another officer pushing the lunch trays. I watched her fat ass jiggle beneath her tight ass uniform pants while she handed the cell next to me some disgusting looking ass trays with a noodle galosh on it. I made it up in my mind right then that I wasn't eating that shit but when Lilly got to my cell I noticed she wasn't handing me the same pitiful ass tray. No, that lil love struck bitch had brought me and my boys trays with a big juicy chicken breast, broccoli with cheese and mashed potatoes on them instead.

"For you and your boys sexy. I came up here just for you and as long as you show me love I'll show that shit right back." Lilly whispered through the bars as she handed me the trays and I handed them back to my boys.

"Bet baby. I guess you in for the LONGEST, most EXCITING, thrill ride you ever been on in yo life then girl. Cause once Quatty loves, he loves HARD!" I whispered back into Lilly's ear as I whispered through the bars then licked the side of her ear.

I watched her ass shake like the leaves on a tree from the warm, wet sensation of my tongue. I had that bitch in a bubble of bullshit when she skipped off smiling at me.

"Dammmnnnn. Big homie on these hoes." Lil Click said laughing once she was gone as he bit into his chicken breast then turned to give Big Moe five.

"Hell yeah, lil cuzz on his shit. Pimpin just in him. I taught you well young nigga. Keep that hoe on a string until you ready to pull her in. But remember, these hoes can't be trusted. That's how I fucked up, trusting a hoe and not my mind. Your job is gonna be to get something besides the trafficking we finna have on the bitch. Get something else you can hold over her head, that way you know she can't cross you without crossing her damn self. You do that and you can ride this shit until the wheels fall off." Big Moe said as I laughed and gave him dap because I intended to do just that.

I told him how I intended to use Lilly to get my message across to Pooh, payback Officer Wallace, and possibly move our dope as he looked at me with pride. By the time Lilly came back hours later to get us for work detail and the yard, Moe was sure we were about to take over.

"Hell yeah, all of that can work lil cuzz. WE ABOUT TO RUN THIS JAIL AND EVERYONE IN THE AREA. We just gotta be smart about this shit. Now, me and most of the brothers on work detail right now, but Lil Click going to the yard with you. Y'all watch each other back out there." Big Moe said as he gathered his shit for work detail and handed Lil Click a butch of his own.

"Oh, fasho big homie. I got Quatty back, you know that. Them niggas will get hell today if anything pops off." Lil Click said as he flashed another butch he had sticking in his sock and Moe told us to stay alert.

I nodded my head and told him I was always with the shit as I watched him tuck his butch away and prepare to leave. After that I watched as another officer came to round up Moe and most of the other brothers in the pod before Lilly came back to take the rest of us to the yard. I made sure my butch was secure as Lilly led us to the door to the yard and it opened up from the outside.

As soon as we stepped out and the noise from the dozens of niggas on the yard filled my ears, I knew why Moe was telling me to stay alert. There were cliques of niggas tucked off everywhere and everybody was loud as hell, trying to be seen. I mobbed with Lil Click over to the bench by the gate with my hands down my pants and on my butch. I was ready for whatever the staring, whispering ass niggas around me wanted to do. Once me and Lil Click got to the bench I sat down with my backed pressed against the fence so that no one could get behind me. I knew the game.

I knew that if you were caught slipping even for a second a nigga would creep up on ya and stick a butch in your back. I wasn't about to let that shit happen though. That's why I just sat there quietly with my back on the fence and eyed all the bitch ass niggas who looked my way. I was barely even listening to Lil Click as he gave me the rundown on all the niggas in the yard.

"Yeah these bitch ass niggas mad because we got the power in here. Last week a nigga tried to poke Durty up in the showers but they didn't know that nigga a beast just like Big Moe. He beat one of them bitches to death with his bare hands and threw him down the fucking shoot. After that the two other niggas bowed all the way the fuck down. Hell, one of 'em even took the charge. That's why these niggas don't like us, because they know we wit the shit." Lil Click said as he laughed and gave me dap while I stared down this big, tall, red nigga with a mouth full of golds.

The nigga was sitting at least 15 feet away from me across the yard but he kept his eyes on me from the time I walked in. For a minute, I thought he was on that gay shit and I'd have to kill him just for the thought, but when Lil Click saw where I was looking he immediately told me wassup.

"Oh, that nigga really don't like us. Well, specifically YOU." Lil Click said as I turned to look at him quickly before I turned back to the nigga.

"What the bitch ass nigga don't like me for? I don't even know his hoe ass." I said as I sucked my teeth and glared at that bitch with malice.

Lil Click quickly told me that the nigga's name was Juice and he was a Vice Lord who rolled with Big Dip. He told me that Juice was one of the niggas who were waiting for me to hit the floor so he could take my head off.

"Yeah, the nigga said he was getting you on sight big bruh, so you see I'm ready." Lil Click said as he casually bent down and took his second butch out of his sock then stuck his hands in the front of his pants like mine were.

I sat there and stared at the nigga who said he was going to take my life as I thought about why the nigga wanted to kill me.

"Over the word of a bitch? So, this nigga in some shit he knows nothing about all on the word of a lying, stanky ass bitch?" I asked Lil Click as he shook his head yes and anger surged all through me.

I felt like old, reckless Quatty instantly as I sat there and watched that nigga smirk. It was like he thought I was scared or some shit as he sat and smiled while he told the niggas around him to look at me. What he didn't know was that I was a goon, a real reckless, heartless ass nigga when provoked. He had brought that side of me back to life trying to stare me down like a pussy. He had the game so fucked up and he found that out quick.

"Oh, so the nigga said he got me huh? As soon as he see me huh?" I said to Lil Click as he shook his head and laughed while I slowly stood up and he followed.

"Well bet then. This bitch ass nigga ain't gotta wait. I'm gonna bring this shit to him." I said as I quickly began to mob towards Juice with my hands still stuck in my pants and on my butch.

I got halfway to the nigga before a commotion bust out on the other side of the yard and we all turned to see what it was. Two, old junky niggas were wrapped up in a full tussel by the gate in full fight mode over who was getting what dope. That was enough to get every officer on the yard's attention as they all filed over to the fight. I just stood there with Click by my side and watched both of their asses get sprayed.

"That was a bullshit scuffle there. Them niggas smoke together so that had to be a distraction for something else." Lil Click said beside me when what it was a distraction for suddenly popped into my mind.

I turned back around to look at Juice again as I told Lil Click it was a setup but it was too late. By the time I looked at Lil Click and then back in Juice direction that bitch and four more niggas was right there in our face. All I had time to do was back up just out of his reach as he swung his butch in the direction of my head and missed me by an inch. That was his fuck up though because it was on as I caught my balance, pulled up my butch, and put that hoe through his chest.

Within seconds it was a full brawl as Juice's big ass wrapped me up and I continued to batter that bitch with my butch. I stuck his big ass with precision every time I moved my hand but that didn't make him let up on the death grip he had on my neck. That nigga was choking my ass so hard that I saw stars as I glanced over and saw the other four niggas beating the fuck out of Lil Click.

I yelled for the few other brothers on the yard to aid and assist us as I summoned all of my strength and suddenly lifted Juice big ass up over my head. Everything and everyone on the yard seemed to stand still as I hoisted the big, 250-pound bastard up over my head and dropped him on his back with my butch still stuck in his chest. Without hesitation, I reached down and pulled my shit out of his chest before I stuck it back into my pants and stomped Juice face in. I had that bitch down there gurgling and flapping around like a fish out of water when I suddenly felt something pierce my back. It hit me hard and fast and I instantly knew that I had a butch in my side.

That didn't stop me from jacking with those four other niggas though so I did what I do best. I jacked with them niggas, holding my own, for a couple of minutes until somebody kicked me in the back. That blow sent my ass flying forward and directly on to my face. As soon as I hit the ground I jumped back to my feet as the niggas tried to kick and stomp my ass to death. They had me fucked up though because I refused to die like a bitch.

Instead I pulled my bloody butch back out and poked one of them niggas up as the C.O's finally noticed the fight and called for the riot team. I couldn't even worry about that though as two more niggas came over to help my ops and I found myself outnumbered again. With Lil Click still on the ground moaning and bleeding from his back I knew I couldn't win as I stared the five niggas I still had to fight down like the bitches they were.

"What you pussies wonna do, huh? You want me nigga? Well, come get me!" I yelled as they all suddenly attacked and I tried to fight my way out of the corner.

I took a dozen blows to the head and neck as I fought my way through the crowd and tried to make it to the gate. When I got within arm's reach I heard one of them yell for the other to cut me and I knew I was in trouble. I turned around expecting a butch to the heart but instead all I saw was this big nigga with dreads and golds as he smiled and slumped niggas.

I mean this nigga was like the grim reaper as he made his way through the crowd, knocking niggas out with one punch. That was enough to get me back with the shit and I grabbed the closest nigga to me and tried to break his fucking neck. I slammed that bitch so hard on the pavement I heard his bones crack as the crowd that had gathered around us cheered. Me and the nigga with dreads quickly worked them pussies out and soon we were the only niggas standing with blood all over us.

"Quatty. Quatty give me the butch... and yo shirt." The dread head nigga suddenly said as we watched the riot squad prepare to come in.

I had no idea who that nigga was at that moment but I knew he had saved my life so I had no problems doing what he said. I quickly handed him the bloody butch and took off my shirt like he said as he handed them off to a nigga standing by the door. The nigga quickly stashed the bloody butches in a pipe on the yard before he handed me and the dread head nigga clean shirts.

"Put this on lil nigga." Dread head said as I did just that then we both laid down on the ground, face down before the riot squad could even get to us.

We laid there with our hands behind our heads and listened to the pussies moan while dread head laughed. I looked at that nigga like he was crazy because he was really amused by the damage we had done. I wondered who the fuck that nigga was at that moment, but at the same time I was glad he was on my side. I guess that was written on my face too because as we laid there he looked at me and answered the question I hadn't even asked.

"Oh yeah, nigga I'm Durty, yo cousin's lil homie. I think you know my old lady too, she a bad ass, shit talking goonette named Yada." The nigga said as I finally realized he was the dope nigga Big Moe was partners with.

He was also the same heavy nigga Yada was holding down on the outside and knowing how loyal his bitch was I knew I could fuck with Durty.

"That's wasup big bruh. I heard a lot about you from Moe and Yada. Nice to meet you nigga, even under the present circumstances." I said to Durty as we both looked over at the bloody niggas the riot squad was pulling away.

We watched them wrap a few niggas up in blankets and I knew right then they were gone. I couldn't do shit but close my eyes and pray that I wouldn't have more murder charges added on to what I already had when it all was over.

"Don't worry lil nigga. We wasn't even in the fight, my C.O. will make sure of that. You just keep yo mouth closed and let them take you to the hole for this lil 24hour bid because tomorrow all of this shit will be forgotten. Trust me lil bruh, we straight. I been through this many times before and every time I get off. You wit me so you cool, lil Click is too. Them niggas ain't though." Durty said laughing as he eyed another nigga the guards were pulling away with holes all in his chest.

I just laid there in silence as Durty's laughter rang in my ears and C.O.'s ran over to snatch our asses up. The guards punched and shook the fuck out of me as they asked what had happened but I didn't say shit just like Durty said. I just let them bitches lead me to the hole behind Durty and then throw my ass in a cell. Just like Durty said we were in there all night, talking and bullshitting through the vents.

We had our shit down pack by the time the C.O. came to let us out at two the next afternoon. We didn't know shit and hadn't seen shit is the only thing we told them when they questioned us about the fight. That was enough for them to release us back to our pod and the jail moved on like any other day. It wasn't like they gave a fuck about some ole convict ass niggas killing each other anyway and that was apparent from their lack of enthusiasm in finding the people who had stuck seven and killed two. We walked back into the pod the next day as heroes having took out all of the VL squad in our part. The G's showed us love too as they shook us up and offered us everything they had.

"Maine y'all niggas fucked them bitches up. We Vice Lord free in this bitch now. All hail the twin hittas. These niggas like real hitmen round this bitch. They was out there poking niggas and knocking they fucking heads off." one gangsta said to Moe as he met us at the door of our cell.

He stood there with this big ass evil grin on his face as we walked in.

"You good Quatty? I heard you got poked." Big Moe asked me as I walked into the cell and lifted my shirt to show him the bullshit ass wound the poke had left behind.

Lucky for me that the pussy who stabbed me didn't have heart because he had barely broken the skin. That Juice nigga wasn't so lucky though because I had bodied his big ass.

"Yeah, I'm good big cuzz. This shit superficial. The bitch didn't do shit but clean it and put this bandage on it when I got to the hole. That Juice nigga wasn't so lucky though, was he?" I asked Moe as I pulled my shirt back down and plopped back on to my bunk.

I watched as Big Moe got up and walked over to the door to look out before he responded.

"You sholl know what to say lil cuzz. That nigga wasn't lucky at all because you bodied his big ass. Now them bitch ass niggas ain't got no leader in here and I got a hit on the rest of them bitches. They gotta answer for this cause Lil Click still in the fucking infirmary with a fucking laceration to his liver and a few broken bones. I gotta get my fucking lick back behind that." Moe said as I saw that determined and deadly look he had even back when we were kids return to his eyes.

He told me of his plans to get the other niggas who were in the brawl knocked off as I sat there and thought about how close to death and doing life behind bars I had gotten. That shit was heavy on my mind as I listened to my niggas joke and play while they lit blunt after blunt. Durty and Moe talked to me about the business and how untouchable all of us could be together as I sat there and listened but didn't really pay them any attention. I kept finding myself in one fucked up situation after the next and every time it came down to a bitch. The same bitch. That knowledge had me fucked up in the head and in no state of mind to make life altering decision like linking all the way up with Me and Durty in the dope game.

I mean at that point, I still wasn't ready to jump all the way in the game when I didn't know what my future held. That's why I didn't agree to anything they said, I just sat there and smoked as I nodded my head. The next day though, the decision seemed to make itself as I went in to see my lawyer and the first thing he did was plop a fat ass letter from the U of M addressed to me down on the table.

"Your fiancée brought this by the office to me Quatty." L said as he sat back with a disturbed look on his face.

I wasted no time ripping that bitch open and reading over the words I dreaded but knew were inevitable.

*Quaderious Jones we regretfully inform you that you have been expelled due to illegal activity,* was the only thing I read before my little hopeful ass world came crashing down around me. I quickly balled that shit up and threw it in the trash can by the door as L continued to tell me about my case.

"I know that was a hard blow my nigga, but all hope ain't loss. You'll be out of this bitch soon as soon as you can get with the Pooh hoe. Focus on that lil bruh, not this other shit. It's their loss, not yours. You a young, smart, ambitious young nigga. You can still turn all this around and live a happy, square ass life. That's if you handle business now. Get Pooh on the phone and get her to say what we need her to say at the preliminary hearing. At this point my guy, that's our only hope." L Whispered before he packed up his stuff and stood to leave.

"You right bruh and now that's my main focus. I'm finna get me some money then get the fuck out of here. Fuck everything else." I whispered back before I dapped L up and we both walked towards the door of the lawyer room.

"Okay, well I will see you next time Mr. Jones." L said loudly in his sophisticated lawyer voice just as we stopped in the doorway.

I thanked him for all of his help as he quickly slipped me a small piece of paper wrapped in plastic and I tucked it into my cheek.

"Pooh been calling my office. Some kind of way she found out I'm representing you and wants to talk. Call that number bruh. I know the hoe ain't worth none of the bullshit you been through but your freedom is worth swallowing your pride. Do that! 12." L whispered quickly before he motioned towards the waiting guard to let him out.

I thanked him again before he walked away and stood there in a daze as the officer opened the gate for L to leave and Lilly came out to get me. I walked back to the pod led by Lilly feeling different than I had left. Gone was that hope I held in my heart and the rest of the compassion I had left. I walked back into the pod that afternoon broken, angry, and ready to jump with the shit. That's exactly what I did too as I told Durty and Big Moe I was down as soon as I walked back into the cell and we started our come up.

# Chapter 4

The first couple of days that followed the brawl on the yard and me receiving that fucked up letter from the university, I unleashed all of my pain and anger on any stupid nigga who dared to cross me. By then Lil Click was out of sick bay and I was back in that I don't give a fuck state of mind that changed my life the first time, that night Nut got killed. I went off on niggas for even looking at me wrong and Lil Click and me beat a few bitches just because they were the op and in the yard in MY section. I was out of fucking control because on the inside I was in agony knowing what my decisions had cost me. I had lost everything I worked hard for because of a simple-minded bitch who just couldn't let go. I had thrown away my future for the love I had for one woman. A woman who deceived me.

Sitting behind those four, dirty gray walls I had nothing but time to think about that shit and analyze whether any bitch was worth all that was gone, or my happiness for that matter. For the life of me I couldn't answer that so I guess I started taking that slick resentment out on the females closet to me, and Lilly was the perfect victim. Right after I told Durty and Moe I was in on business they tested my abilities by sticking me on the bitch. Moe wanted to see if my pimpin was as strong as I said it was so one day he told me to get Lilly to bring me in some cigarettes and cigars just to test the water.

At first I was apprehensive because I still hadn't really did anything to make the bitch risk her job and freedom over me yet. However, after she came in that Friday smiling and giggling all up in my face, I knew I could bag her ass with little or no effort. That bitch melted in my hands at that moment as she giggled an

"Well good morning beautiful, smiling all bright and shit. Your smile warms me up girl. Makes a nigga feel free, like I'm outside, under the sun with something soft and thick pressed up against me. Damn. Lilly." I said in my deepest, most Denzel like, seductive voice as I flashed her my famous Charming Quatty smile.

That bitch melted in my hands at that moment as she giggled and pressed her DD's up against me quickly before she casually walked over towards the control room. I smirked to myself as I glanced around quickly and noticed no one else was on duty and in the pod with her. I nodded my head at Moe and Lil Click as they stood in the door to our cell and laughed before I glanced over to spot Lilly. I smiled and did a little shimmy, mocking Moe and Lil Click, when I saw her wink her eye and the turn to go into the room, leaving the door open behind her.

"I got this shit handled my niggas, watch this." I whispered to them as I casually strutted pass them while I kept my eyes on everyone else in the pod.

No one was paying me any attention besides the two laughing muthafuckas standing in my cell door, so I quickly slipped into the office with Lilly and closed the door. As soon as I was inside Lilly wasted no time making sure I knew what she wanted. I stood with my back to the door and bit my bottom lip at the bitch as she immediately began to unbutton her shirt.

"Ayeeee, hold up lil mama. Pump yo brakes now." I quickly said as she walked over to me and pinned me up against the door using her body.

"Hold up what QUATTY? What I gotta wait for? You want me just as much as I want you so why the fuck we waiting?" Lilly asked as she pressed her pelvis up against me and wrapped her arms around my neck.

That bitch was like a cracked-out octopus as her hands touched damn near every orifice of my body in 60 seconds. She even tried to kiss me in the mouth as she whispered my name and grinded her hips in unison. She had the game fucked up though so I quickly turned my head and did a gentle football jug to get her off of me. I knew the game, hell I had heard it a million times from Big Moe.

"Hoes don't get the dick for free. Make that bitch break herself before you even pretend to dick her down. Hoes don't realize it young nigga, but they the biggest tricks in the fucking world. A bitch gotta pay me for everything; conversation, time, convenience, and just to be in my fucking presence. Don't let these hoes get a second for free. Remain in control at all times my nigga." I could hear Big Moe say as I stepped just out of Lilly's arm reach and turned on my ice grill.

I could see that I had to assert my authority with Lilly off the muscle and let her know that even though she was the one in a power role, I still had the control and she was going to do what I said if she wanted the benefits. I knew that's what had to be done, but I also knew I had to be subtle about it and coax the bitch's ego while playing off her insecurities at the same time. Moe was more of the brute leader who beat his hoes into submission. I didn't want to be that nigga.

Even though Pooh had taken me through hell and back I still didn't think I could be that nigga to physically abuse any female. Even a hoe like Pooh. That's why I took a more psychological approach and tried to play off of morality and self-respect to keep that lil hot pussy hoe back and in check. Hell, she had me scared of the pussy from how hard she was throwing it at me so I slowed her lil red ass all the way down.

"Hold up beautiful let's slow this shit down. Yeah, I want you. But guess what?" I said as I suddenly stepped a little closer and stared her down.

I could see the angry and confused look Lilly had on her face after I shook her off disappear as I charmed her lame ass like a rattlesnake in a wicker basket.

"I respect you way too much to even try to make love to your sexy ass in some nasty ass office. You a queen ma, and a nigga like me gonna treat you as such." I said as Lilly cooed and purred like a happy kitten and I reeled her ass in.

"Besides baby, thugs need love too. Just because I'm in here and been in a world of shit doesn't mean I don't have feelings too. I been burned by females my entire life. I can't just trust my heart and my body with anybody. Especially when she ain't showed me her love first." I said as I took one step closer and Lilly looked up at me with a loving but apprehensive expression.

I could tell she could feel the game coming and the look in her eyes told me she might buck. I didn't care though because I had come too far to turn back and I wanted… nah, I needed to play with that bitch's mind. Hell, I needed to play with her life for that matter. I needed to make some hoe suffer like a bitch had done me.

"If you really feeling me like you say you are Lilly, you'll make life in here a little easier for me. Now, I really appreciate them fye ass dinner plates every day for me and my boys. I know you cook that shit at home and bring it in, and I really appreciate it. But, what a nigga really need is some squares and gars. Hell, maybe even some loud and a burner. That's what I need. See, I'm a boss nigga, inside and out on the streets and I take care of home. If you trying to rock with me, fuck me, or whatever then that means you a part of home so when I shine you do too. In order for me to show that love back though baby, I gotta get my head above water and only a bad bitch can do that. Are you that down ass bad bitch I can count on and build a fucking empire with?" I asked Lilly as I stepped up again and pressed my body against hers.

"Are you." I asked as I bent down and let my breath gently massage her neck and watched her shiver.

For a second I thought that bitch would nut in her panties and empty her fucking purse, giving me everything that she had. However, when she suddenly stood back and took on this stern ass expression I lost all of my pimp dreams.

"Excuse me Inmate Jones but you have to leave this office right now. I will definitely talk to the infirmary about getting you some pain medication for your stab wound. However, you cannot be in this office. This is a warning inmate, next time your ass is going to the hole." Lilly said in a harsh tone as she stepped from behind me and I turned to see another C.O. walking into the office.

I felt relieved as fuck as I told Lilly I was sorry and walked towards the door. Lilly turned her head before she told me to hurry out and then turned her attention to the guard. I lost that feeling of relief then because that hoe's tone and demeanor told me that she was not playing. That's exactly why I got my black ass on.

"Damn, what the fuck happened?" I said to myself as I walked out of the door and to my cell while I cursed at myself for fucking up the lick.

"What happened nigga? Let me guess, you told the hoe you loved her after she put that fat monkey on you, and now she ain't gonna do shit. I told you nigga, cash before ass." Big Moe said laughing as he gave Lil Click dap and we all walked into the cell.

"Nah nigga, that hoe didn't get shit. I had that hoe eating out of the palm of my hand until that other muthafucka walked in. That hoe did a whole 360 then." I said as I plopped down on my bunk and Moe and Lil Click continued to laugh.

I ignored them niggas as I sat there and sulked like a bitch and the whole situation played out in my head. I tried to figure out where I had gone wrong as Moe and Lil Click continued to talk shit, but I couldn't figure out what had happened no matter how hard I tried. Who could though with those fool ass niggas in the room?

"I bet you asked that hoe some like, 'Excuse me beautiful lady but will you be my girlfriend? And while you're at it delightful young lady, would you bring in some contraband for me?" Lil Click said in his impression of a sophisticated voice as Big Moe laughed his fucking heart out. I wanted to fuck both of their bitch asses out for laughing at my failed attempt but that shit was funny as hell. I couldn't help but to laugh and allow those fools to lighten my mood.

"Maine fuck y'all niggas, I had that bitch. That other C.O. fucked me up. Give me one more try and watch me bag that bitch right in you niggas face." I said as I held out my hand to Moe to make the bet like we used to do when we were kids.

"Aite ole nice ass nigga, bet. Let's see you get that bitch. You already struck out once in there loving on the bitch, three strikes and yo ass out." Moe said laughing as he clasped his hand in mine and we sealed the bet and Lil Click bet with Moe." Okay see nigga, now Click in it. You finna owe both of us bruh. It's over for that hoe. She ain't giving yo pretty ass sh--" Moe said and suddenly stopped as I turned to see what he was looking at.

When I turned around I looked directly into the cute face of the thick little guard name Lilly as she signaled for me to come over.

"Hey, I just didn't want you to think I was fucking you over or nothing but I had to cover my ass. I need this job now… to help my man. Ain't that right baby?" Lilly whispered as I shook my head yes and then turned to lick my tongue out at Moe and Lil Click weak asses before I turned back to Lilly.

"Damn right baby. Now, you gone and do what you need to do to make daddy happy. You my bitch. Remember I take care of home." I said before I quickly looked around then leaned over and kissed the patch of skin behind her right ear.

Lilly shivered like she was on the water in Antarctic in a string bikini as soon as my lips touched her skin and I knew I had that bitch wrapped around my finger. My boys knew it too. I could hear Moe telling Lili Click that he had taught me everything I knew as I watched Lilly walk to the cell next to mines and then stop.

"See you in the morning as soon as count clears daddy. Okay?" Lilly asked as I nodded my head then she blew an air kiss before she hurried away. I watched her fat ass bounce and jiggle until she made it all the way to the other end of the tier then I walked back into my cell.

"MY NIGGA!" Big Moe said as I walked in and he jumped up off the bunk to shake my hand.

"I knew you would get that hoe. She was yours from the first time you saw her I bet. Now nigga, let's see how this shit goes. If this hoe is as slick as she looks and as smart as we need her to be, tomorrow will be the beginning of something bigger than any niggas in jail have ever done. I'm talking about a million dollar a month fucking business niggas. We can be bigger than Nino from behind concrete walls. Y'all niggas ready?" Big Moe asked me and Lil Click as he stood up and held out his hand. Lil Click quickly ran over to give Moe five and tell him he was in.

"Nigga, full speed ahead. What I got to lose?" I said after I got off my bunk and went over to shake Moe's hand.

"Bet. Let's get rich then." Moe said and we kicked our plan in motion.

That entire night I continued to flirt with and love on Lilly in simple, none weak nigga ways. Every time she would walk past me I would whistle slightly under my breath then blow her a kiss when she looked back. I kept my eyes on her the whole day and hers were on me as well. She bent over or brushed up against me with her titties or ass every chance she got, showing me she was down. That was enough confirmation for me so after my shower and right before Lilly got off at 8 pm, I went in my cell to sleep.

Moe, Durty, and Lil Click were out of the cell when I got in there so I quickly laid down to enjoy the quiet. I wished I hadn't done that though because as soon as the silence set in my thoughts began to roam. My mind wondered back to that slip of paper L had given me with Pooh's number on it. I quickly lifted up the top of my mattress and stuck my hand into the slit I cut in the mat and pulled the slip of paper out. I read over the number twenty times until I knew it by heart forwards and backwards then I got up and flushed the slip of paper just like I wanted to flush Pooh's crazy ass out of my life.

The last thing I wanted to do was call her and have to ask her looney ass to lie for me. That would be nothing but another thing she could hold over my fucking head and make me pay for the rest of my life. Hell no. I wasn't ready to do that. Not right then anyway. Surrendering to the bitch who made my life hell was not a priority when I had so much other shit going on. That's why even though it was hard, I pushed it to the back of my mind. I closed my eyes and thought about hurting Pooh and making her feel everything I felt. I fell asleep with revenge on my mind and hope that my hell would soon be over without me having to make a pact with the devil.

That's exactly what Pooh was too, the devil. She was evil as hell, just a big ball of crazy wrapped in a gorgeous shell. She was a beautiful nightmare in my dreams too as she came to me suddenly while I lie asleep on my bunk. I saw her thick, beautiful, evil ass standing in the door of my cell looking bad as fuck in an officer's uniform yet she had Lilly's face. That shit freaked me out too, so much so that I woke up in a cold sweat right before morning wake up call. I sat straight up in the bed and glanced around the cell kind of confused and still freaked out by my dream as it flashed in my mind.

"Lilly and Pooh. Two nothing bitches who want a nigga for various fucked up reasons and ain't worth shit. I guess if I get one, I get them both." I said as the answer to my dream suddenly popped into my head and I got up out of bed to prepare for my day.

I had my shit and was standing at the door waiting on them to roll the bars as soon as count was called. Moe wasn't far behind me as he and Lil Click took their spots for count and they cleared us fast. We all hurried to the showers and did what had to be done quickly before we rushed back to the cell. Them niggas were more anxious than I was as they rushed through the pod, but they had me fucked up. I was the basketball star and the nigga getting the package so there was no way they were beating me. I kicked shit into overdrive and sprinted past them niggas quicker than they could blink. I was the first nigga to walk in when we got back to our cell so I was the first to spot the bulge in my pillow.

"Ummm what's this? What did my Lilly bring daddy?" I said in a mocking tone as I stuck my hand into the pillow case and pulled out a carton of cigarettes, two cases of cigars, an ounce of mid, 20 oxy's, and a fucking smart phone with her burner number already programmed in it.

"Dammmnnn." I said as I turned towards Moe and Click with the burner in my hand and they came over to see what all I had.

"Hell nah fool. That hoe brought you the complete real nigga starter kit. Oh, yeah my boy. This hoe a keeper. You gotta ride this shit out Quatty. If you gotta give that lil bitch some dick, do that shit. She showing you she ready to go over and beyond. I got rubbers so don't worry about that. You just keep the hoe happy to keep us paid. Now, Monday we gonna need a big shipment brought in and we need her to help. Put that hoe up on game and get her ready." Moe said as I nodded my head and then he began to say something else.

"Oh nigga, don't forget to get something on that bitch that will hurt her way more than it hurts you. Or better yet that will only hurt her and not you. Find something that is not related to drugs at all that was happening way before you got back here. That bitch was down at 201 for two years before she moved here so I know she got history. Find that shit and hold that shit until you need it. We gotta be smarter than these hoes nigga. Ain't nan hoe worth even more loss." Big Moe said as I agreed and set out to reverse the hell in my life.

I flirted and got close to Lilly all weekend while trying to keep my mind off of calling Pooh. Even though I had that important mission in the works along with regular calls to Tinka and the occasional visit from her or my homies, I still couldn't think about anything other than the phone call I knew that was inevitable. When Monday rolled around I had shaken off that Pooh monkey on my back and was ready for Lilly.

Right after count I snuck into the control room when Lilly was manning the pod alone and did what had to be done. I think she expected it too because when I burst into the door she was sitting in her chair with her legs gap wide open and tongue out as she rubbed the top of her breast through her shirt. She was like one of those naughty prison guards in an old flick, trying to seduce the inmate. I smirked to myself as I looked at the bitch's lust drunken eyes and she got up and walked over to me.

"I remember what you said last time my king so I know I won't be able to feel you inside of me. I only have fifteen minutes anyway, but that's enough time for me to show you how my king is treated though." Lilly said as she suddenly dipped down to her knees and pinned me against the door as she stuck her hand into my pants.

As soon as she grabbed my monster and then rubbed her face across my crotch I felt that muthafucka grow fully erect in a matter of seconds and ready to do damage.

"Damn daddy, you ready huh? Umm, that's what I like to see." Lilly said as she quickly whipped my dick out of the front of my TDOC jogging pants and attempt to put it into her mouth.

I wasn't that far gone in lust though because I caught that shit and quickly pushed her face to the side. I heard her sigh as I bent down and got the rubber Moe gave me out of my sock, opened it, and slipped it on.

"Now I'm ready my Lilly. Safe sex or no sex baby. Remember that." I said as I rammed my erect 10-inch dick down the bitch's throat.

She took that shit like a pro too. She didn't even gag when I hit the dougie in her mouth and jiggled her uvula. Instead she just worked her cheeks and tongue, massaging my shit and making her mouth wetter than a glass of water. I damn near bust right then as she moaned and massaged my nuts in a circular motion while she twerked her ass on the floor. I felt like I was on set shooting a fucking rap video and not in jail in the damn commander's office. Just thinking about how I had changed my luck with bitches in a blink of the eye and the power I held in my hand made me even more excited as Lilly continued to deep throat my dick. Before long I was busting in her mouth then pulling her up to me as I laid kisses on her neck.

'Damn girl. My Lilly. Baby, you the one." I whispered in her ear before I slipped my tongue inside her ear lobe and my hand into her pants.

In seconds, I had my index and middle finger deep in her juicy, warm center helping her reach that organism she chased like a fix. I dug my fingers deep inside of her and licked her neck until I felt her body begin to jerk against mine.

"You my bitch huh? Huh? Aren't you Lilly?" I asked her as I continued to batter her g-spot and kiss all over her face, neck, and ears.

"Yes!" Lilly panted as she held on to me for dear life and grinded her hips while she fucked my hand back.

"Hell yeah you my bitch. And as my bitch you do what daddy say right?" I whispered into her ear before I gently licked then bit the lobe then smacked her hard on her ass.

Lilly's lil freaky, always ready ass shivered and moaned so loud I had to cover her mouth as I continued to finger her and whisper demands.

"So, you gonna go to the address on the piece of paper I put in yo pocket, pick up the package and bring it in to me tomorrow right? Right? Or are you just down for fucking and not getting real money and building something with yo king?" I asked as I suddenly stopped moving my hand, took it out of her pants, and left that ass hanging on the edge of ecstasy.

I folded my arms and leaned against the door as I watched her pout and whine for me to finish what I had started.

"Okay daddy, I'll do it. I'll go get whatever it is and bring it to you. I ain't scared of shit. I been hitting this crooked ass system. Doing this with you ain't shit. Hell, I bought two houses, four cars, and sent my kids to private school the past four years off the money I clipped from 201. You better ask somebody papi, Lilly gets her money by any means necessary. Now, come on over here and finish what you started." Lilly said as she walked back up on me and pinned me to the door.

That was all I needed to hear. I knew I had just what I needed to ensure Lilly's loyalty for as long as I wanted it. That's why I had no problem finishing what I started and leaving her lil freaky ass spent and lifeless in the chair. I damn near patted myself on the back as I scrolled out of the door with confirmed delivery for the next day.

"The package will be in the worker's shed for Moe to get it by afternoon count tomorrow. I got you daddy. As long as you got me." Lilly whispered as I walked out of the door gloating at my success.

My bitch wasn't lying either because from that day forward she granted my every wish. Not only did Lilly bring us in a huge shipment of drugs every week, but I flipped shoes and phones like I was on the town. That bitch kept me straight and full no matter what and I still had done nothing but let her suck on and hold the dick. I just couldn't bring myself to fuck her even though she was fine and down for a nigga. My heart was still with Tinka and I felt guilty as fuck for cheating every time I sat back and thought about it. Even with the fists full of cash I was stacking and sending home to my family, I still felt like I was fucking up by doing worse than I was mad at Tinka for. That's why I had made it up in my mind that I was going to tell her the truth and then live with the consequences of my actions.

One month after my little scheme and affair with Lilly began and over $700,000 in dope money was at my disposal, one Saturday morning I headed to visit ready to ease my guilty conscious. I intended on telling Tinka everything as soon as I saw her and making sure she understood I had done it for us. However, when I walked into the visitation room and saw her big, round belly, glowing face, and all of the people she had brought with her, I knew it wasn't the time or place to spill my guts.

That's why I swallowed back that shit like a real nigga and fought my conscious the entire visit. I was able to push that nagging feeling in my heart to the side as Tinka introduced me to her sister Belle, nephews Shawn and Ty, and Niece Kasey. After hugging everyone and giving my nigga Ghost some dap I helped Tinka into her seat and she began telling me all that was going on. She told me how the phone calls had continued and she had a slip at work so she had invited Belle and the kids down to stay with her. I could tell she wasn't sure how I felt about her whole family living in the house, but what she didn't know was that I was relieved.

I liked the idea of her sister and the kids being there to help and watch over her when I couldn't. That's why I told her that was a good idea and watched that huge ass smile spread across her face. After that Ghost told me about him and Belle's relationship and we jokingly planned a double wedding. The whole visit I didn't think about shit but the people in front of me. At that moment, I realized what I was missing at home and I wished more and more that it all could be over. I still wasn't ready to call Pooh yet though, but that boost came at Tinka's next visit.

Two weeks after visiting with Tinka, Belle, Ghost, and the kids, Tinka came back unexpectedly on her own, and I knew something was wrong from the second I laid eyes on her. Her usually on fleek hair was all over her head and I could see that her eyes were red. I almost ran across the room without being cleared when the guard took my cuffs off. I just wanted to see what was wrong with my baby and take all of her pain away. Business was good as hell, I'm talking almost millions good, but that didn't mean shit if I didn't have Tinka. Her and my baby were the only reasons why I was going so hard knowing I had no career to fall back on. That's why making sure she was okay was my top priority as soon as the guard said I was clear to start my visit. I ran over to Tinka in a flash and quickly wrapped her plump ass in my arms as she cried her eyes out.

"What's wrong baby? Tinka, what is it? Talk to me baby. I love you Nicole. Please." I said before I kissed all over her face then the guard yelled for us to sit down.

I ignored his bitch ass even when he gave a second warning because I wasn't letting go until Tinka did. When she did I helped her into her seat before I sat down and gave her my attention. She wasted no time either as she told me how Lay-Lay had taken over Pooh's role as psycho terror and started up the harassment again.

"Phone calls, letters, broken windows, they even tried to jump Belle in the yard. You know my sister ain't no hoe though so she busted at them bitches but they got away." Tinka said as she cried and I told her it would be okay.

"That's not the worst of it though Quatty, them hoes started to fucking with the babies. Shawn, the quiet one of Belle's kids, got jumped by Pooh son and six other niggas after school yesterday and he fucked up. Now our families at war and more muthafuckas getting hurt. Hell, Ty and Ghost caught one of the grown niggas who jumped Shawn this morning and beat his ass half way to death. 12 got Ghost too baby so he'll probably be back up in here soon. Belle fucked up behind that and I'm fucked up too because I don't know what to do. I can't be going to war with hoes carrying my baby but I ain't no weak bitch either. Belle and Yada been holding me down but what about when they not there? What if them hoes catch me slipping Quatty? I can't lose another baby." Tinka cried as I reached over the table and wiped her tears away.

My mind was moving a mile a minute trying to process all of the shit she had just said. I couldn't believe those maggot ass hoes were still at it and dragging kids into that ghetto shit. Right then I knew what I had to do to end it all even though I didn't want to do it. I couldn't stand to see anyone else hurt knowing damn well I could stop it by one call to Pooh and telling her I loved her. I knew that was what had to be done so I swallowed my pride and planned to do it.

"Look baby everything gonna be okay. Ghost know what's up. That ain't no murder so he getting right out and will be back there to help protect you. In the meantime though, call my mama soon as you leave and tell her to give you $20,000. Take that and y'all go get another lil low key place to lay low in until I get home. All of this shit gonna be over soon baby I promise. All of this ghetto shit. Just trust me Tinka. Okay?" I said before I told her I loved her and gently kissed her lips.

We talked for a little longer until they called for the end of visit. I stood there patiently and watched my baby walk out before I left headed to the phones. I fought that voice inside of me that still said not to call as I got the eighth place in line for the phones and stood there weighing my options.

"Get yo ass out of line Jones, you just left visit. No phone too. Let these other sorry sacks of shit have some joy too you selfish bastard. Now, move bitch before I send you to the hole." Wallace yelled from behind me as I turned and stared his big ass down.

I hated that nigga with a passion and I couldn't wait for the day to get my revenge. I started to make that day, the day and punch that hoe in his throat. However, when I looked around and saw all of the other officers on standby I knew that was a battle I wouldn't win. That's why I just shook my head and laughed as I walked back to my pod and daydreamed about the day I'd get him and Pooh.

"Soon both of you bitches will feel my wrath. That's my word." I said to myself as I went into my cell and waited on my time to shine.

# Chapter 5

The next morning I woke up hyped, focused, and ready to fulfill my plan. That visit with Tinka the day before was still on my mind and weighing heavy on my heart so I knew I had to do something. That something was get with Pooh and finally put an end to all of the chaos we had been living. I didn't want to bow down to that bitch but I knew I had to at least pretend to until I could get out. That's why I ignored that nagging feeling in my heart which had returned and got my ass up and got my day started. Lil Click and Big Moe were already up and gone for kitchen duty before I even left the cell to shower. I wasn't worried though because during my four months of chaos being held without even a preliminary hearing, I had proved I wasn't the nigga to fuck with. Especially, with Durty's big crazy ass lurking, and waiting on some shit to pop off. I nodded at him as I let Lilly lead me to the showers and he nodded back before he got up to guard the shower door.

"You got goons on deck don't ya baby? That's that king shit I like." Lilly said smiling as I quickly undressed and her amused expression changed to one of lust.

I watched her big ass eyes sweep down my body until she stopped at my fully erect, throbbing dick.

"Damn daddy, it's like that? I need that in my life." Lilly said as I laughed at her and shook my head while stepping into the shower stall.

I knew exactly what she wanted. She wanted a nigga to dick her down and boo her up on some wifey shit. The only problem was, I already had a wifey, and Lilly nor no other bitch could compare to her. I couldn't tell her that though because I needed her, and deep down I think I was sort of beginning to have feelings for her too. I didn't want to but hell, over the months I had been in jail she was the closest thing to me; handling my business, brining me shit, and just holding a nigga down. She was the ride or die bitch I had asked her to be, I just didn't love her like I loved Tinka. I didn't want to hurt her anymore though, that's why I didn't plan on using that information I had on her. I wished I could get that same dirt on officer Wallace though so I threw out the bait and waited to see if Lilly would bite.

"I know you need it baby and soon as I get up out of here you're gonna get it too. All of it." I said as I stepped back through the curtain with my rock hard dick in hand and soap suds all over my body.

I smiled as Lilly walked closer to me while biting her bottom lip. She looked like she would eat my ass alive as she rubbed down my wet chest and fucked me with her lust filled eyes.

"I'd wait on that for a life time." Lilly said as I licked my lips, leaned over and kissed her on the corner of her mouth then went back in to finish my shower.

I turned to see her still standing there frozen with the feel of my touch still on her skin. I knew she was still wide open and that was the perfect opportunity for me to apply more pressure.

"In the meantime though, baby I need to get rid of a few problems. One in particular, WALLACE. I hate that big bitch ass nigga and I gotta find a way to get him. Ole Uncle Tom bitch. He be coming at a nigga all wrong, trying to treat a nigga like a boy. I gotta get that bitch but I can't find shit on him." I said throwing the bait out and just like I thought, Lilly let me reel her in once again.

I could see her brain moving as I talked and when I finished she gave me the ammo I needed to fuck Wallace off and put him right where he said I'd always be.

"Oh, fat black ass Wallace? That big, faggot bitch. Hell, I got plenty dirt on him. He been laundering money longer than I have. And the pussy got a sweet tooth for young, white boy booty." Lilly said and I felt like I was going to faint.

I saw the whole plan take shape in my mind as I thought about how I would not only get his fat ass flapped for the money but I'd also get him caught balls deep up in some little, poor defenseless, white boy's ass. I wanted that big bitch on the other side of those bars so he could see how it felt and I was going to get Lilly to do it for me.

I continued to get information out of Lilly as I washed away the troubles from the day before. Once she told me everything I needed to know I began to groom her for the take down we were about to pull off. I told her to get in touch with her homegirl who still worked at 201 and get us as much solid information on the money scheme as she could. I even thought of a way to cover her ass by making it look like the funds she had stolen were really stolen by Wallace too.

By the time I got out of the shower I had that part of the plan secured with Lilly saying she would call and get the information ready for me that day. That was all I needed to her to put my ass on cloud nine and have me leave the showers skipping and shit. Durty couldn't do shit but smile when he saw me come out of the shower smiling and walking like I had just got released. I could tell by the sly ass look on his face when I walked past him that he thought I had fucked Lilly. What he didn't know was what

I really had done was fucked Wallace and I wasn't done yet.

"We finna fuck this nigga life up baby, you just stay on top of that info. We gonna get that bitch 50 years so he can see how it feels to be treated like a fucking dog. That's not all though. I want everybody to see what that trick ass, shit packer really is so right before I go to pretrial I'm gonna need you to set something up for me. Just stay ready to move when I say so. It's time we dangle some bait in Wallace face and catch his faggot ass on tape catching it. You get my drift?" I asked Lilly once we had gotten back to my cell and I stood in the door staring at the new, young, scared ass white boy who had just come in. Lilly smiled an evil smile that let me know she was totally with the shit once she followed my eyes to the boy.

"Oh yeah, I got you King and I'm on it. You can always count on me." Lilly said before she quickly blew me a kiss and disappeared to the control room.

I stood there and watched her fat ass sashay away before I turned my attention back to the little white boy. He sat there looking scared as hell as various niggas in the pod planned their attack on him. I couldn't let that happen, at least not before he played the most important role in my plan anyway. That's why when Durty made his way over to me to ask what I had done to Lilly to make her fall in love, I quickly told him to spread the word NOT to fuck with the white boy.

"Maine tell these niggas he is off limits until I say so. Nobody bet not touch him or that's they ass." I said as Durty shook his head then turned to leave.

He took three steps before he turned back around with his face scrunched up and asked me why protecting the white boy was so important.

"That lil nigga our insurance policy big homie. Trust me. It will all make sense to you in a minute, but right now just go spread the word." I said to Durty before I turned and went back into my room to finish getting ready.

I thought about the phone call I was about to make and all the shit I had going as I finished dressing, secured my shit in my cell, and then walked back out into the pod to meet Durty. I told him all about my plan to fuck off Wallace as we walked to the phones and he laughed.

"Hell yeah gangsta, I like that plan. Fuck that big loose booty ass nigga. He gonna see how being on this side of the bars feel. And I tell you this, regardless of how much time they give his big ass. He will never walk out of those doors again. I'll make sure of that." Durty said before he gave me dap in the phone line and then laughed his way back to the pod.

I stood there in line and thought about what I would say to Pooh as the line got short fast as hell. I ain't gonna lie, my fucking heart was beating in my throat by the time I made it to the front of the line and I was about to call. I was scared as fuck I would say some shit that would piss Pooh off and she would fuck me off so they could keep my black ass forever. That was my only fear and that fear fueled that nagging feeling in my heart and made my damn knees buckle as I dialed the number.

I had to channel that cold nigga on the inside of me and ice up my heart to stop my legs from shaking and get my shit together before she answered. I knew that bitch was like a bloodhound and could sniff out a weak nigga from a mile away. Hell, that was how the bitch had kept me cornered for so fucking long. However, shit had changed and by the time she finally answered the phone and accepted the charges, I was sure she could feel shit had changed from the ice in my voice.

"Yeah, wasup Pooh?" I asked flatly as she squealed and shit into the phone. But I was not fucking impressed.

"Quatty. Quatty baby is that you?" Pooh yelled into the phone like she was so fucking excited to hear from me.

That bitch acted like she hadn't put me through hell by trying to kill me, killing my baby, trying to murder my bitch, and a gang of other shit. That psycho bitch was still so deeply submerged in that fucking fantasy world she had built for herself inside her mind, she still wasn't ready to face reality.

"Quatty baby, I miss you so much. I'm sorry shit went bad but you know it's because of how much I love you. I've always loved you Quaderious, since we were kids and I'll never, EVER stop." Pooh said and I felt the ice on my heart harden a bit more.

That bitch still wasn't accepting the fact that I had moved on because in her fucked up mind, nothing had changed. I had to shake my head and look at the phone, wondering was that hoe really that crazy or just dumb as hell. I wanted to ask her that shit too but I caught myself, remained cool, and said the shit I felt I had to.

"Maine Pooh, it's good to hear your voice and all and know that you okay. But so much shit done happened shawty. I don't even know what the fuck to say. You hollering you love and miss me and shit, but WHY THE FUCK AM I HERE MARIAH?" I asked losing my cool for a second as I held the phone away from my face and growled.

The niggas in line behind me stepped back when they saw me about to spaz the fuck out. They didn't want me to take my fucking wrath out of them and I can't say I blame them.

"Maine this bitch gonna make me merk her ass." I said as I growled and Durty walked up behind me.

"Bruh I know you want to curse that bitch out, but think of the bigger plan. Kissing a little ass momentarily is worth your freedom lil homie. Even if that BITCH ain't." Durty whispered as I nodded my head and turned back to the phone.

I knew that nigga was right, I had to swallow my pride and do what the fuck I had to do. I was glad his big ass was around to watch my back and keep my head on straight when my other homies weren't around. Durty had talked some sense into my hot headed ass so I was ready for that bullshit Pooh was preaching by the time I put the phone back up to my ear.

"Quatty I'm sorry, I really am. I know these words don't mean shit though. That's why I need to see you. I need to see you so you can see that I'm serious and that I'm very, seriously sorry. I promise I will make this right. Just put me on your list and let me come see you tomorrow baby. I promise I will make this right. Please Quatty." Pooh begged as I smirked at the phone, happy to hear that bitch grovel.

I knew it was all bullshit though because just below that sweet, submissive, loving surface was her rotten, evil, trifling ass core. That bitch was the best actress I had ever seen, just ghetto and crazy as fuck. I pulled a page out her book that time though and gave that hoe all her fakeness right back.

"Aite baby, I hear what you saying. You gonna have to show me though Pooh. We been here many times before so forgive me for not believing shit you have to say. I am gonna give you a chance though. I'll give you a chance to right your wrongs. After this though Pooh, if you burn me. I'm done FOREVER. Anyway, I'm putting you on the list. Be here when visit start. Oh and by the way, I love your crazy ass too." I said in a cold, flat tone as Pooh squealed in delight and I quickly hung up on her ass.

Although I had won and had Pooh ready to do what I said after I gave her what she wanted, I still felt defeated as I mobbed back to my cell. When I got back inside Durty, Big Moe, and Lil Click were sitting on the bunks smoking and undoubtedly talking about me. I knew them bitches were when I walked through the door and they all started laughing. I jacked Lil Click up by his collar and damn near flung him out into the pod and off my bunk when I walked in and they kept laughing.

"Why you weak ass niggas in here cackling and shit like lil school girls. Ole foofoo ass niggas?" I said as they continued to laugh and Lil Click got up off the floor.

"Maine bruh, you always so fucking violent. And strong as hell. Damn, you would think the nigga would be weak with all the bitches he got. Ole Bill Bellamy looking ass nigga." Lil Click said as he fell on the bunk laughing, trying to give me dap.

I didn't dap that weak ass nigga or laugh with them bitches, always playing and shit. I was still mad at myself and in my feelings for having to talk sweet to Pooh. My niggas didn't give a fuck though, they kept fucking playing.

"Hell yeah lil cuzz, teach me how to be a player. Ole cassanova ass nigga." Big Moe said as I looked at him before I threw a pack of noodles at his head like a fucking missile.

I wanted to laugh like a muthafucka though and I did a little on the inside. However, I couldn't really enjoy the moment because the visit with Pooh the next day was on my mind. I wondered how that shit would go and how I would be able to keep myself from choking the bitch the entire time my niggas continued to check me.

"Real talk though Quatty, Moe the fucking pimp and you got MOE hoes than him. I know you a silver tongue bastard, ole pretty boy, athletic ass young nigga, but you got these hoes going like you got a golden dick. We just saying put us on ole Deuce Bigalow, Male Jigalow ass nigga. We wonna slang dick to a herd of bad bitches too." Durty said and began to laugh as everyone's head snapped around to look at him.

None of us could believe that nigga had said a joke when he always was so damn violent and on go. He laughed all the time true enough but that was only when he was hurting muthafuckas. That's why it was at least a 10 second pause after he said that shit and started laughing before we all joined in. That shit right there completely cleared my mind and relieved that stress. That and a talk with my boys on how to deal with Pooh followed by a good home cooked meal from Lilly and some fye ass head made my day go by lovely as fuck.

The next morning I woke up still happy, but in a more serious and determined way. I was ready to get the shit over with and get on with my plan. That's why wakeup call didn't even have to wake me up because I was ready and at the door when the bars rolled once again. Me and the homies went off to the showers with Lilly's fine ass leading and got that shit done, efficiently and quickly.

When we got back to the cell we chilled for a minute and got high as I made a call to Tinka. Something had happened the night before in my dream so I had another sudden urge to clear the air. I told my niggas to step out for second when the phone began to ring and they all left to shake niggas down for their debts. When Lil Click's ole playful ass finally made it out of the door Tinka finally answered and I knew my plan to confess was out the window.

"Hello, baby? Quatty you ok?" Tinka said in that sweet and caring tone of voice that made me love and miss her so much.

Regardless of anything that had happened I knew she loved me and that's why I couldn't tell her shit. I had to lie to protect her heart, at least long enough for us to be together again.

"No baby, I'm good. Why you think something is wrong?" I asked Tinka as Lilly walked into the room and I told Tinka to hold on.

I put the phone on mute before I looked up at Lilly's little thick ass while she stood by the door with her hand on one hip and a big envelope in the other. I could see a hint of jealousy in her eyes as she stared at me and I knew she must have heard some of my conversation. I didn't really care though because it was a fact that Tinka was my wife. That was a part of the game I had sprung on Lilly and she acted like she was cool with it. However, as she stood there and shifted from one leg to another and stared at me, I wondered how cool she really was.

"Wasup my Lilly? What you got for me baby?" I asked casually, like shit wasn't happening.

I wasn't about to offer an explanation to that bitch when she wasn't my woman and she knew that already. That's why as she continued to just stand there with a slight smile on her face and a little hurt mixed with jealousy in her eyes, I picked the phone back up, checked to see that Tinka was still on hold and on mute, then began to check my text messages. I acted like that bitch wasn't even standing there. I let her have her little thot-trum until she was ready to act like a mature idle hoe. After about four seconds she learned her lesson and walked over to my bunk to throw the envelope besides me.

"Now was that so hard? Damn Lilly. What's wrong?" I asked as I stared up at her and she suddenly smiled.

"Nothing baby, but I won't lie, for a second I walked in and got jealous. I know who Tinka is though and I know what she means to you so there's no need to be jealous. As long as I have my place in your heart that's all that matters. Besides, Tinka fine as fuck. Hell, even pregnant. Keep on it's gonna be a menaj going on when you hit the time. Remember, I love bitches as much as you do." Lilly said before she licked her tongue out and winked at me then turned and left the room.

I watched her ass jiggle as she left and got a little light headed. I damn near got a shiver behind that shit, just imagining both her and Tinka in bed with me at the same damn time. I don't think my heart could take that shit and from the way my dick was swelling up at just the thought, I don't think it could either. My thoughts of a threesome threw me all the way the fuck off and I damn near forgot Tinka was on the phone until she started pushing buttons.

"Quatty!" Tinka yelled as I took the phone off of mute and put it back to my ear.

"Wasup baby? Sorry about that. I had to get off the phone because the C.O. came in here." I said as I heard Tinka sigh on the other end.

"Oh, ok baby. That's what I was asking about before you got off the phone. I was wondering why you were calling me from a cell when you said they were for business. I thought something had gone wrong." Tinka said and I quickly calmed her fears and got to the good shit. We talked for a while about the upcoming court dates and I all but guaranteed her I was coming home. By the time we were ready to get off the phone my baby was happy and I was too. I told her I loved her after that and she said it back before I hung up.

"I think I love you too." Lilly suddenly said from the door and I looked up directly into her big, beautiful, sincere eyes.

I don't know why but I felt deep down I had some love for Lilly too. That's why it was nothing for me to quickly lie to her as I got up with the envelop in hand.

"I love you too lil mama, and I'll love you more if this is what I think it is." I said while opening the envelop and pulling out its contents.

Inside, there was loads of records I along with several jump drives, pictures, and receipts. All of them were pieces of evidence I could use to bring down Wallace and ruin his fucking life.

"Yeahhh. Baby, you did that shit. We got that bitch now. Come here girl." I said as I wrapped my arm around Lilly's waist and pulled her deeper into my cell just out of sight.

Before I knew it, I had leaned down and kissed her right on those big, juicy, peach lips. The taste of pineapple and the cool sweet scent of mint quickly filled my nose and mouth and we locked in a deep kiss. When it was over I suddenly walked away like nothing happened and began to put everything back into the envelope. I looked out of the corner of my eye to see Lilly still standing there pinned against the wall by an imaginary me with this bewildered look on her face.

"Aw yeah, my Lilly. I love you so much girl." I said and that time, I don't think it was that much of a lie.

The more Lilly helped me, the more I felt like I had more than the usual one-sided type of love for her. Hell, I knew she loved me just as much as Tinka did after all the chances she took daily. I guess that's why it was evitable I began to develop real feelings for her lil, sexy, freaky, loyal ass.

"Oh, but I love you more king. Now come on and go to your visit." Lilly said as I handed her back the envelope and told her to keep it until I can back from visit.

I felt confident and happy as a muthafucka as I scrolled into search and then into the visitation room. I lost some of that happiness though when I walked through the door and saw Pooh sitting there at the first table in a wheelchair. She was still fine as ever with her crazy ass, but it was a sad, sympathetic type of beauty.

For a second I almost forget how evil the bitch was and how quick she changed like the weather. However, by the time the cuffs were off me and I walked over to the table, all of those bitch boy feelings had faded away. All I could do was see flashes of the tragedy and pain that bitch had brought into my life, and all I wanted to do was get the visit over as soon as possible and be rid of that bitch for good. I sat down at the table across from Pooh as she wheeled forward a bit like she wanted a hug but stopped when she saw I was not trying to offer one.

"Wasup MARIAH?" I said as I looked into her big, beautiful tear filled eyes and she tried to reach across the table to grab my hand. I wasn't having that shit though. Even though I knew I had to play along to get the hoe to withdraw her statement, I wasn't about to let her put her fucking paws on me to do it. That bitch had done too much for me to forgive her like that and she knew it.

"Oh, I'm sorry Quatty. I know you don't want me to touch you. But just hear me out baby. I'm so sorry for all of this and I'm determined to make shit right. I got word the preliminary hearing in another month or so, and I plan to withdraw my statement. I'm going to tell them I said it was you being vindictive, and I guess that wouldn't be a lie. I did a lot of shit to you out of malice and for that I am truly sorry. I know that doesn't change shit but maybe I can make up for it." Pooh said as tears streamed down her cheeks.

I looked directly into her eyes as she talked and for a second I saw old Pooh. Buried deep beneath the games, drugs, niggas, lies, and chaos I saw that beautiful smart girl I would have given the world for. That girl was gone though and I knew that. Just like that old, easy to manipulate Quatty was gone. I had nothing but ill feelings for Pooh as she sat there crying in a wheelchair wanting me to feel sorry for her stupid ass. I didn't though. All I felt was a need to hurt her worse than she had done me. That gave me the motivation to pull off an Oscar worthy performance of my own and trap that bitch like she had done me.

"It's okay baby." I said as Pooh's eyes got big as hell. She couldn't believe I was being nice. In her mind, she had won the game.

"We all do shit we don't mean when it comes to those we love. Just know none of that shit can ever happen again and we good." I said as Pooh shook her head and I continued.

"Anyway, now that is out of the way, I really need you to make that statement. Call my lawyer when we leave and gone get that ball rolling. After that, maybe we can work on starting over." I told Pooh and she smiled so brightly through her tears it was like someone had turned on the sunshine. We talked for a few minutes later about the kids and everything else that had happened. She told me how the bullet Tinka hit her with ruptured her bowels and she was forced to shit in a bag. I felt kind of sorry when she said that but I knew she brought that shit on herself. By the time the guard called the last five minutes of visit I was tired of hearing Pooh's sad ass song so I quickly jumped up to go.

"Quatty, wait a minute baby. I need to ask something else." Pooh said as I was walking away and I turned back around to face her.

The look on her face told me she was with the shit and whatever she was about to ask was going to be fucked up. I already knew it before she opened her big ass mouth.

"So, are you still with Tinka? If so I don't know if I can do that." Pooh said snapping back into her old evil self but I was ready for that shit. I stepped closer and then squatted down so that she and I were eye-to-eye.

"Baby, I'm single until you show me we can be one again. I ain't got time for love when I'm trying to get my life back together. Help me get my life back baby. Then we can work on us." I said before I kissed her gently on the forehead and prepared to go. I saw her wipe a tear away and smile before she nodded her head okay.

"Say she was never worth it Quatty, then I'll know it's real." Pooh said as I shook my head. I knew that's all the bitch wanted to I stroked her ego.

"She was never worth it, but you are." I told Pooh as she smirked before she rolled away and I turned to walk away.

"And bitch you ain't even worth the waste in your bag. Cripple ass hoe." I said as I walk over to the door and right into Lilly's waiting arms.

She gave me a quick hug before I got in the front of the line and we waited on everyone else to end their visit.

"Who was that? You're sister or something?" Lilly asked as I looked at her like she was crazy.

I knew what that was about. I knew that meant Lilly was lick jealous but she had nothing to worry about with Pooh and I let her know that.

"Aw that's the reason why I'm here. That's the rotten bitch who gets me locked up every chance she gets because she can't have what you got." I said to Lilly as I leaned over towards her ear.

"That's another muthafucka we gotta get rid of but we can worry about her at another time. First, I gotta get out this bitch." I said as Lilly sucked her teeth and looked towards the door like she was going to chase after Pooh and run her evil ass down a hill.

I could tell right then it was levels to Ms. Lilly and part of me wanted to explore them all. I liked that flicker of fire in her eyes as she stood there thinking.

"Aw yeah that bitch gonna learn and I'll be the one to teach her. I ride for mine baby, believe that." Lilly said snapping out of her hate filled haze and turning her glance towards me.

I smiled at her before she winked her eye and started getting the rest of the niggas coming to the door in order. One nigga called himself going to skip me and get first so I grabbed his bitch ass and slung him back.

"Maine bitch ass nigga, I know you lost yo mind touching me cuzz." The tall, black ass nigga said as he ran back up like he wanted to jack.

I couldn't help but to laugh at his dumb ass, picking a fight with a fucking beast. I was just about to punch that bitch in the throat and have his ass fitted for a trach when Lilly came out of nowhere and hit his ass across the back with her nightstick and broke him the fuck down.

"You're going to the hole inmate." Lilly yelled as she bent over and cuffed his ass then waved for another officer to come get him.

I smiled with pride at my bitch being all gangsta as she looked up and winked at me. She made a nigga blush a little behind that and by the time she walked back up to lead the line I wanted to dick her down right there. There was just something about a boss bitch who wasn't scared to throw them hands. That shit turned me on and I couldn't hide it as I walked behind Lilly and whistled.

She switched that fat ass even harder then and by the time we made it back to the pod she had my dick rock hard. I damn near started power walking trying to get back to my cell, grab my shit and shower to wash away my lust. However, Lilly wouldn't let me get away that easy because before I could get away she called me back. Her eyes swept up and down my body quickly as she noticed my hard dick.

"Ummm I see daddy like that huh? You like a bitch to take charge?" Lilly asked as she whispered in my ear then looked me in my eyes.

"Well get used to it because I'm your ridah until you say so and like I said. I ride for mine to the end, right or wrong. I got you baby. Now go handle that or you want me to?" Lilly asked seductively as I looked at her like, bitch yeah.

She smiled when she saw that and told me to hurry up. She didn't have to say nothing but a word because before she could finish I was sprinting to my cell to get my shit. Lil Click, Durty, and Big Moe were in the cell when I got in there waiting on me to tell them what was up.

"What it do Quatty? How it go with Pooh?" Moe asked as I quickly gave them the rundown on my visit and the info I got from Lilly.

"So, I got the rotten bitch on track, my main bitch down and finer than ever, and my lil ride or die on her shit. Life good for a mack right now gangstas, so I can't complain. Now if you dry dick ass niggas will excuse me, I got a warm, wet mouth waiting on me in the showers. Ole ashy dick bastards." I said to them niggas as they all laughed and told me to fuck myself before they take my hoe.

My homies continued to talk shit and laugh until I left the cell, but I just laughed and ignored them. I could still hear them when I met Lilly by the door. That didn't stop me though, I just kept going and walked straight into some of the best head I had in a while. I left the shower feeling light as fuck and the big as steak, potatoes, broccoli and apple pie Lilly brought us for dinner made me feel even better.

I went to sleep that night feeling like there was hope to finally end my chaos and live a good life. Over the month and a half following that day, my light feeling only got lighter. I still had Pooh fooled, Tinka in love, and Lilly ready to do anything for me. Shit was even good on the streets after that with all harassment stopping from Pooh and LayLay. Pooh figured she had won so she finally left Tinka alone. That's exactly what I had hoped she would do so I was happy to see she had.

Soon it was the day before my preliminary hearing and I was completing the next part of my plan. That morning I got all the papers Lilly had given me on Wallace and put them in a new envelop for my lawyer with a note attached telling him to read it asap and get the info into the right hands. Next, I wrote a letter to Pooh, telling her what a rotten bitch she was and how I had won, and that she wasn't worth it. I put a note on the front of that envelop too that told my lawyer not to give it to her until I was walking out the door. Once I did that, I handed them off to Lilly before I returned to my cell to chill with my niggas.

"Tomorrow the day they release the beast and then Durty you won't be far behind. When we hit these streets its hell to pay for niggas on the outside and in here. That Wallace bitch first, he will be coming in as we leave out and I want you niggas to give him hell. It's our time my niggas. It's L.O.A. and we on our way to the top. Just watch!" I said as my niggas agreed and I stamped that shit in my mind.

I had a feeling that was the beginning of something beautiful as I looked at my homies smiling faces. If I could have only foreseen the pain that would come along with it, I could have saved myself some heart ache.

# Chapter 6

The day of my preliminary hearing I woke up anxious and excited as fuck. I was so ready to get the shit over with and get on with my life, nothing else matter. It was so real and so within my reach I could almost taste Tinka's sweet, juicy pussy on my lips. When I got up Lil Click and Moe were already up, the doors had already rolled, and they were gone. I thought I had overslept after I saw that so I quickly jumped up and grabbed my shit for a shower. I was just slipping on my shower shoes with clothes in hand when I suddenly felt a small, soft hand in the center of my back.

"Today is the day that they free my king and help me start an important part of my life. For six months, I have laughed with you, helped you, and grown to adore your tall, sexy, smooth ass. I guess what I'm trying to say is Quatty, today you will get your papers to free your body from this cage, and I hope it will also be the day you free my heart. Don't let what we have be a bad memory like this place. Just know that I'm only a phone call away. Whenever." Lilly said as she got on her tip toes and whispered in my ear.

Her warm, sweet breath caressed my neck and face, and sent chills up and down a nigga spine.

"Wherever. And HOWEVER, you want me king. I'll be on call. Now turn around and let me give you this fire court day head before my help comes in, and your breakfast gets cold." Lilly said before she kissed me gently on the neck then turned me around to face her.

Lilly's eyes were so seductive and beautiful as she stared at me and bit her bottom lip. I couldn't even contain myself as I ran my fingers down her cheek then cuffed her chin before I helped guide her down to where she needed to be. In seconds, Lilly had my massive wood in her hand, had slipped on a rubber, and stuck it in her mouth as she did those wonderful tricks with her tongue I had grown to love. I couldn't help but to feel a little weak in the knees as Lilly deep throated my dick then pulled it out and let the wetness from her mouth run down on it.

When she sucked it back up, deep throated my dick again, and cuffed my balls at the same time, I thought I had died and went to heaven it felt so damn good. I closed my eyes as I leaned back against the bunk and let my head rest on the bed. The wetness of her mouth and the light moaning she was doing had my ass going like a porn star. I couldn't even help it when I grabbed two handfuls of her hair and began to fuck her face like an animal. That shit felt like wet cotton as I got balls deep down her throat.

I could tell that Lilly liked that shit too as she moaned even more and I looked down right into her eyes. Just seeing her big, beautiful eyes staring up at me in that compromising position almost made me bust right then. I stopped that shit though as I closed my eyes and slowed my pump all the way down. Instead I began to grind my hips and move from side to side showing Lilly what that dick really could do if it was in that pussy.

I hit the dougie on that bitch once again and when I did I suddenly could hear muffled laughter coming from the pod. I looked up just in time to see Moe and Lil Click crouched down by the door with phones in hand laughing their asses off. I flipped them bitches the bird then smiled as they continued to tape and hold their mouths as they laughed. I know Lilly heard them fools but she just kept sucking anyway. That's why I figured, fuck it, if she didn't care I didn't give a fuck either.

I cranked my dougie back up on that bitch then, folded my arms, threw some gang signs and everything as Lilly continued to suck. My niggas ate that shit up from the door as they pumped their fists and bowed like I was the king. That's what I felt like too being sucked up by a bad bitch in my cell. I guess at that point Lilly got tired of me showing my ass so she pulled another trick out of her bag and broke my ass down.

Suddenly she took a page from my book as she slowed her pace all the way down, gripped the shaft of my dick firmly and began to suck while flicking her tongue and turning her hand gently from side to side while she stroked gently back-and-forth. That shit was like a combination of sensations that were all designed to steal a nigga's soul, which is exactly what I think they did. My knees buckled like a muthafucka after only three sucks and I had to hold the bed with two hands just to keep my balance.

I could hear my niggas laughing again as I continued to hold on with my eyes closed and knees shaking. Lilly was on some real Pinky shit with moaning and ass twerking as a bonus. Before I knew it I couldn't take anymore and my nut hit me hard and fast like thunder. Lilly felt it though so she quickly pulled the condom off and positioned her mouth under my dick just as I started to nut. What I saw her do after that was like a child waiting up to see Santa on Christmas night and finally catching that fat bastard with toys in hand. I was amazed like a muthafucka as Lilly drunk down my babies like fine wine, massaging my dick and balls and steady drinking until the last drop. She had me lifeless as fuck by the time she was done and I fell back on to the bed. I looked up at her as she wiped the corners of her mouth then sucked her finger while smiling.

"How you feel now daddy? Ready for court?" Lilly asked playfully as she spinned around slowly while she rubbed her hands across her fat ass.

"Maine, how I feel right now? I'm ready for any muthafucking thing. A nigga could die after feeling that little piece of heaven. You a bad muthafucka girl." I said to Lilly as she patted herself on the back and laughed at me.

"Well thank you my king, and that's only for you. Despite what the rumors may say. I have only fucked with one other nigga in jail and he was my baby daddy so don't let the lies fool ya. You different though daddy. I can see a future in your eyes and I want to be a part of it. Just remember I'm always here. Now do you want your breakfast before or after your shower?" Lilly asked before I told her after and she blew me a kiss as she left the room.

"I'll be back after I do this walk around to take y'all to the showers then I gotta lock you back down before my help comes." Lilly said as she walked out.

"So get y'all giggling, creepy asses up and get ready too, Walker and Johnson." Lilly said to Moe and Lil Click as they called themselves hiding behind the pillar and she began her cell check.

I quickly pulled my clothes up and got up on shaky legs as Moe and Lil Click stormed in still laughing.

"Fool you dead. How you walking and shit?" Lil Click said as he came over and poked my shoulder and I pushed his dumb ass away.

"Hell yeah lil cuzz. On the real. I saw yo fucking soul leave yo body fool. That bitch sucked the life out of you. AND I GOT IT ALL ON TAPE! Check it outtttt!" Moe said laughing as he and Lil Click showed me the footage they had.

Those perverted bastards had taped it from the beginning, not missing a fucking second. I stood there for a minute with them and laughed and enjoyed the moment. Then I suddenly thought of Lilly and what that tape could do to her and I asked them to get rid of it.

"Delete that shit y'all for real. Lilly good." I told Lil Click and Moe as Moe told me I was crazy.

I told them how down Lilly was and how I didn't want to hurt her as Moe did an imitation of a man playing a violin.

"Fuck that lil cuzz. You need a big ass insurance policy when fucking with anybody in law enforcement. Hell, with anybody in general. Look how useful that knowledge on Wallace fat ass is. Now Lil Click you erase yo shit because that was just for recreational purposes but lil cuzz I ain't erasing mine. I'm sending this shit to my email and my sister back up email just in case then I'll erase it off the phone." Moe said as I walked over and watched him do it.

I felt what my big cuzz was saying but at the same time I didn't want to fuck off Lilly. I was relieved when I saw him erase that shit off the phone so I turned so we could leave.

"Look lil cuzz, don't forget how I got here. Hell, and how you got here too." Moe said as I nodded and Lil Click stepped up.

"Hell, how I got here too. Remember I beat that nigga because of the bitch." Lil Click said and Moe agreed.

"Nigga, remember how we all got here, BECAUSE OF A BITCH! Don't make the same mistakes twice. Pooh and the love and trust you once had for her landed you in this bitch. Don't let Lilly and that sweet mouth be next. Now, I ain't saying she ain't a good bitch. I'm just saying, you never know. Every bitch ain't worth the chance bruh. Remember that!" Moe said as I turned and dapped him up then we walked out and right into Lilly.

I could tell from the look on Lilly's face that she had heard some of what Moe said because no matter what I did she wouldn't make eye contact. When we got to the shower door I fell back and let my boys go in first so that I could talk to Lilly. I didn't want my bitch feeling bad and getting ideas of turning on me. That's why I was ready to do damage control as I stood in front of Lilly and bit my lip while looking down into her slightly sad eyes.

"What's wrong with you my beautiful Lilly? Your smile didn't meet me at the door so I know something is wrong." I said as Lilly tried to force a smile, but I could see right through that shit.

I sucked my teeth and turned my head to the side to give Lilly a, yeah fucking right look, as she shifted nervously from foot to foot. We stood like that for a few seconds until Lilly finally realized I was not going to give up and went ahead and told me.

"I just heard your cousin say you can't trust every hoe and that every bitch ain't worth it. I don't want you to feel like that about me Quatty. I don't ever want you to question my love or loyalty because baby I'm down for you. I know you didn't say it and it may not even be how you feel. Hearing it just put me in my feelings. That's all." Lilly said as I saw tears well up in her eyes.

I quickly pushed them back where they came from when I grabbed her hand in mine and used the other hand to grab her chin.

"Hey hey hey, stop that now Lilly. You know niggas say any damn thing. From day one you have been my ridah so there is no question in my mind as to where your loyalty lies. What another muthafucka thinks doesn't matter to me Lilly. Seeing your beautiful ass smile is the only thing that matters. So, baby, dry your pretty little eyes. Daddy love you girl." I said in my Billy Dee voice before I suddenly leaned down and kissed Lilly lightly in the corner of her mouth.

I felt her shiver when the electricity from our kiss surged through her body. I felt that shit too but I didn't let her know it. I just stepped back, smiled at her and left her there in the doorway shaking with a smile on her lips.

After my shower, I came out and Lilly was still standing there, damn near in the same position. I couldn't help but to laugh with my niggas when we walked up on her and scared her half to death. She was still trapped in a lusty haze that had her zoned out until we were right there in her face. By then it was too late though because we saw she was too far gone.

"Very funny gentlemen now come on. "Lilly said laughing too as we followed her back to our cell.

After that Lilly locked us back down and her help came on duty minutes later. Me, Moe and Lil Click sat in the cell and smoked and talked for the few hours after that while the rest of the jail woke up, dressed, and prepared for breakfast. By the time breakfast was over and my court time drew near my nerves began to kick in and I got up to pace the floor. Moe and Lil Click joked saying I looked like a bitch at the WIC office waiting on the vouchers as I paced, but I didn't give a fuck what those niggas said. All I cared about was getting to court and making sure Pooh did what she was supposed to.

My biggest fear was that the bipolar bitch would get in there and at the last-minute change her mind to stick with the story. That was the thought that had my ass pacing and wouldn't let me stop until Lilly brought in the new, black, Hugo Boss pants and jacket, with crisp white shirt and shoes she had bought me. I dressed still in a daze as my niggas told me I looked like one of them faggot niggas on GQ magazine.

"Quatty look like he going to sale some high class, old white bitches some dick, not go to court." Lil Click said laughing as Moe joined in on the laughter.

"Hell yeah. The Gangsta Gigolo back on the prowl." Durty said laughing as he walked into the cell and everyone joined in.

We all laughed and tripped for a while until Lilly came back in and told me it was time to go. I dapped all my ganatsa's up as they showed me love then walked out into the pod with Lilly. All of the other brothers in the pod showed me love and wished me luck as Lilly led me out of the pod and to the bus.

"Good luck baby, even though I KNOW you don't need it. Next time I see you, you will be a free man. Free to fuck! Later my king." Lilly whispered right before I got into the van then I sat down and watched her walk away.

The entire ride from the Penial Farm to the Shelby County Justice Center I went through a whirlwind of emotions that kept me on edge. Not knowing how shit would turn out had me in an uneasy state that I just couldn't shake. That shit intensified too when the van pulled up outside of the building and the officer yelled for us all to pile off the bus.

I swallowed down the lump in my throat and summoned my inner real nigga as I got off the van with a brave face and marched inside with my head held high. Even though inside I was worried as fuck that Pooh would have a change of heart I didn't show it. I looked cold as ice and sexy as fuck as I strolled in shackled from head to toe with six other niggas. My lawyer, L, met us at the door and I was allowed to sit and talk to him as everyone else was processed in to see their public defenders.

"You're up first Jones so get that shit together quickly. It ain't like yo bitch ass ever getting out anyway." Wallace said laughing as I sat on the bench with L and glared up at his ass.

If looks could have killed, I would have murdered his big punk ass ten times. They couldn't though so I knew I had to kill that bitch with my power so I smiled up at him before he walked away and I turned to L.

"Wasup brother, tell me the info I gave you on that bitch was enough." I said to L as he smiled an evil smile like mine as he pulled a stack of papers out of his brief case.

I watched him riffle through them like a kid with all the cheat codes to the game, all excited and shit. I couldn't help but to get excited and shit too because I knew what he had to say was what I wanted to hear. I was right too.

"Maine, was it enough? Nigga, what you gave me finna blow the lid off a multimillion dollar scam that's been going on for years. I hollered directly to my nigga, a brother, in the FBI and he jumped on this shit. They coming to get that big bitch at 7 am Sunday, which will be the exact time you are released if everything goes well today." L said and I sat back and sighed, relieved as fuck.

"So now all we gotta do is get in here and get this shit done. You ready bruh?" L asked me as he stood up and I stood up too.

"I'm always ready big bruh. I stay ready to keep from having to get ready." I said to L as he told me that was what was up and we walked over to the guard to enter the courtroom.

Inside the court room, to my surprise, everything went as I hoped. I walked in to see Tinka, Ghost, Peedy, Yada, Belle, my mama, and my sister sitting in the front row to show me support. Their smiling faces warmed my heart as I was led to the defense side and sat down. Once seated L and I went over a few pieces of information as the judge spoke with the court officers.

After a few minutes the door to the courtroom opened and Pooh rolled in with the state prosecutor and Lay Lay's ratchet ass in tow. The glares those bitches got from my family and other supporters in the room were crucial so much so I bet them bitches could feel the heat on their skin. I threw daggers at them bitches with my eyes too until Pooh suddenly turned to look at me. When she did look at me all of my anxiety faded because I knew I was as good as out. Pooh blew me an air kiss as Lay Lay rolled her eyes and I smirked at her trick ass.

That was enough to put me on cloud nine and fill my mind with nothing but happy thoughts of all the shit I would do when I got out. I barely paid attention as the state gave their weak ass evidence and my lawyer ate that shit up in my defense. I didn't even have to say shit because by the time the defense called their star witness to the stand to make her initial statement, their case was already over. Pooh rolled up there with a nasty expression on her face from the jump and as soon as the prosecutor asked her what happened that day she destroyed their whole case.

"I don't know what happened that day. I just said what you told me to." Pooh said as everyone in the courtroom gasped and chatter broke out everywhere.

L and I looked at each other and smiled as mayhem erupted in the court and the judge banged his gavel.

"Ms. Watkins, so you are saying you were cohered into making that statement? Are you saying Mr. Jones did not commit the crimes he is being accused of?" The judge asked as everyone stared at Pooh and she sucked her teeth.

For seconds, she sat there sucking her teeth and thinking as she stared into my eyes. It was like she was daring me to fuck up so she could change her mind. I wasn't that stupid though so I did what I knew she wanted me to do. I quickly blew her a kiss when no one was looking and sealed the deal.

"That's exactly what I'm saying. I was on medication when they came to the hospital all hostile and told me what had happened. I didn't remember anything, not even the fact I had got shot. They told me what to say. I know Quaderious didn't do it though because he was across town at his girlfriend shop. I talked to him right before I pulled up to the scene of that murder at my house and then I got shot. It had nothing to do with Quatty." Pooh said as everyone gasped again and the prosecutor threw her pad on the desk.

"Oh, I'm sorry Ms. Long, I just couldn't say what you wanted me to say anymore and ruin someone's life." Pooh said to the prosecutor as chatter continued to rise in the courtroom and I laughed.

After a few seconds of gavel knocking after that the judge had had enough foolishness and he made sure everyone knew it.

"SHUT UP!!" He yelled which got everyone in the room's attention.

It was so quiet in that bitch after that you could hear a rat pissing on cotton. I held my breath as the judge looked around the room and tried to find the best way to say what was in his head. I guess after a few minutes he gave up on that shit because the next thing I knew he was going the fuck off.

"Everyone in here should be ashamed of themselves, acting like fools. This is a court of law and you will act accordingly or I will lock all of your asses up, attorneys included. Now, you all have wasted my time and the court's time today, bringing this weak ass case before me. There is no evidence Mr. Jones did anything or was even in the vicinity. Therefore, right now I am dismissing these charges and releasing Mr. Jones." The judge said as my family went ham and he banged his gavel again.

I on the other hand was stuck, not realizing what I had really heard. I thought I was dreaming or hallucinating so I asked L what he said and the judge heard me.

"Mr. Jones, what I said was, you are free to go and the city of Memphis apologizes for this inconvenience." The judge said before he got up and left, then I damn near fainted in my chair.

That shit was like music to my ears even though I still wouldn't get out for another day. That didn't matter though as long as the judge said I could leave, that's all that mattered.

"We did it boy. You free brother." L said as we hugged at the desk and my family was allowed to come over and hug me too.

Tinka wobbled over with her big, eight months almost nine pregnant belly and I wrapped her in my arms. I held her the tightest and the longest with my eyes closed as I inhaled her sweet scent. When I opened my eyes, I looked directly into the scrunched up face of Pooh. She looked like someone had snatched her breath as she stared at Tinka's belly and rolled her eyes. I ignored that bitch though as I stepped to the side to dap up L again.

"No, YOU did it my nigga. You did it and I'll never forget it. You got me out of this shit my nigga. You saved my life. It's eternal love bruh." I said to L as I glanced back over at Pooh.

I could see the anxiety in her rising as she continued to look from me to Tinka then down at Tinka's stomach. It was like watching a kid poke a bee hive filled with a swarm of angry bees. Like, you know somebody about to get fucked up, you just don't know how bad. I didn't know either but I quickly found out how bad shit could get when Pooh suddenly yelled out in the courtroom.

"Quatty really? She pregnant again? I love you Quatty. What about us? What about what you said?" Pooh yelled out.

For a second I couldn't believe that shit, I thought it was all in my head. However, when I looked at Tinka and saw this distant, hurt, unforgiveable look in her eyes, I knew I had heard right. Right then I knew shit had taken an awful turn and that was apparent when Tinka suddenly turned and stormed out of the courtroom. My life damn near fell apart right then as I watched the one person I wagered it all for walk away. I felt my fucking knees buckle behind that and so did L as he reached over and grabbed my shoulder, helping me to find my balance. When I felt calm again, I wanted nothing more but to hurt Pooh like she had just done Tinka.

"Now one more order of business." I said to L as he nodded his head in agreement because he already knew what to do.

I watched him as he walked over to Pooh and put the letter in her hand. After that he walked me to the door and I was handed back off to the officers.

"Alright brother, the next time I see you we will be walking out the doors of the Penial Farm to freedom. Stay safe until then brother. You know niggas hate what they can't have. 12 bruh." L said as I told him fasho and 12 back.

I took a deep breath of fresh air before I turned and began to walk towards the van. I was half way on to that bitch and headed back to be released when I suddenly heard Pooh's voice.

"Quatty you lying muthafucka. QUATTY! TALK TO ME!" Pooh yelled from the other side of the fence and I looked at her and smiled before I got on the van.

I could still hear her cursing as I took a seat in the back of the van and the guards prepared to move us.

"They gonna fuck you up bitch. You won't walk out of those gates. I can guarantee you that. Since you still gonna play with me and be with that hoe, let's see if she worth yo life. Fuck you Quatty, you bastard. QUATTYYYY!" Pooh yelled as I laughed and looked out the window to see officers jacking her up.

That was the last thing I saw as the van drove off headed back to the belly of the beast for my last battle before freedom.

# Chapter 7

As soon as I got into the Penial Farm after court I could feel the shift of energy in the air. I was already in slick misery of my own wondering if Tinka would even be there when I got out and what Pooh's evil ass had up her sleeve. At that fucked up time in my life the last thing I needed was that jail bullshit. I knew I couldn't escape it though, so once searched and processed back in I walked to the pod seemingly unfazed with what appeared to be a moving target on my back. Maine shit just didn't feel right and every pair of op eyes I passed were on me. I didn't let that shit rattle though me as I slowly walked to my pod keeping my eyes on my surrounding and the guard's pepper spray. I hated that Lilly wasn't the one there to take me back like she was supposed to be because if she was I knew I'd have access to info and anything else I needed.

I was a hood nigga though so I was going to improvise and just jack the little blonde, weak guard bitch who replaced Lilly if I had to protect myself. If it came down to it, I'd get to that pocket knife Lilly told me she kept in her bra and slice some bitches up. Nothing happened though because them niggas knew what would happen if they caught me alone and my goons found out. They knew we'd burn that bitch down and that's why they bowed the fuck down and let me pass peacefully.

Once in my pod my brothers shook me up and told me to go straight in to the cell to holler at Moe as I stood in the middle of the day room and mean mugged niggas. The looks on their faces told me that all of them pussies had something on their minds, but no one had the nuts to say what the fuck they had to say. Just like bitches, they preferred to talk behind a nigga back and sneak attack and shit but that wasn't about to happen. I was too far in my feelings and close to the edge for a nigga to try me. I bet them bitches could see it on my face too as I sucked my teeth, folded my arms, and smiled at their asses.

I stared down some new nigga who supposed to had been the leader of the bloods, and made that pussy look at his shoes. That shit had me cracking up, laughing all shrill, cold, and evil and shit like Durty's crazy ass. That caught my brothers off guard and before I knew it Lil Click was at my side, pulling me by my arm to the cell.

"Yeahhhh my nigga a free man. Come on maine, fuck them niggas. You know how we move bruh. Get in here so we can give you the business." Lil Click said as we walked to the cell and I stopped at the door to dog those bitches again before I went inside.

Inside my cell; Durty, Moe, Lil Click, and a couple more loyal soldiers had a smoke session going on. As soon as Moe saw me he dismissed them extra niggas and I sat down and waited on them to leave. Durty handed me the blunt and gave me dap as we sat there and watched Moe stand up with a serious expression on his face. When the last extra nigga had left, Moe turned to look at me and he suddenly had a huge smile on his face.

"MY NIGGA QUATTY, MY MUTHAFUCKING COUSIN. YOU FREE NIGGA!!!! You beat a muthafucking murder charge and an attempted murder charge nigga. You the real MVP. So all you niggas, raise yo muthafucking blunts and let's smoke one with the goon! I already paid the guards so we straight. Light that shit." Moe yelled as Durty handed me a blunt and we all lit them bitches at the same time.

I smoked with my niggas for hours until shifts were about to change and Lilly showed back up to help us clear out the smoke. I laid on my bunk and watched her help Moe and Click spray and fan the weed smoke that was going no fucking where as I thought about my life. There I was, finally free, but what the fuck was I going home to? My wife was mad at me and probably wouldn't ever talk to me again and my ex was crazy as ever, ready to fuck up my world. Hell, the only good thing I had going that second was in jail, the one place I was trying to leave. Even though I hated to say it., Lilly was the only female in my life at the moment who loved me unconditionally and that made a nigga feel good.

I kept watching Lilly's ass while she skimmed over the cell to make sure we didn't miss any paraphernalia for the next shift to find as Moe, Durty, and Lil Click left to get rid of shit. She looked sexy as hell in those tight ass pants as she bent over to check under Moe's bunk. I couldn't even contain myself as I jumped up and stood behind her, pressing my dick up against her fat ass. I had never felt her softness so close to me so it caught me off guard when my dick instantly got hard after feeling her soft, fat ass. She giggled as she slowly stood up and I bent down to whisper in her ear.

"I can't wait to get inside you girl. Open that thang up gently like a delicate flower. My Lilly." I whispered in her ear in a smooth seductive tone but for once I wasn't on no Denzel shit.

I really meant what the fuck I was saying as I felt her lust and love all over me. Time and situations had me weighing my options or at least looking at additions. I figured Lilly would be a damn good addition too so I secured my shit. I kissed Lilly on her neck gently before I turned her around towards me and gave her a quick, passionate kiss on the lips.

I could hear her gasp then hold her breath when our lips finally touched and she was still holding it with her eyes closed when I stood back. I had to shake her ass so that she would finally release it and open her eyes again. When she did I saw tears and streaks of love that made some of that pimp shit Moe had been preaching to me melt. I wanted Lilly in my life. No, I needed Lilly in my life and not just for a limited time. I wanted Tinka too though so I had to figured out a way to get them on the same page. I made a mental note to start on that plan as soon as I got out as Lilly finally shook out of her haze and kissed me back.

"I'm even more anxious than you my king, but our time is almost here. Soon we will be free to be together, once you get your house in order. I told you I'm ready to be a family with you and Tinka too. So, you just think about it baby and know that I'm ready whenever you want me to be in whatever capacity. You got a hold on me Quatty and I ain't going nowhere. Now, get ready for this shower so you can get some rest. One more night in hell after this. I need you well rested and safe my king." Lilly said and that last part caught me off guard.

Out of all the time I had been dealing with Lilly she had never told me no shit like that because she knew it was the opposite, niggas weren't safe around me. That's why that statement fucked me up when I thought about the energy I felt coming in to jail and all the fucked up looks I got. None of that shit was right and neither was Lilly worrying about me so I had to find out what was up.

"What you mean be safe baby? Where the fuck that came from?" I asked Lilly as she tried to walk away and talk, but expecting it, I grabbed her hand.

I swung her back towards me and looked her deep in the eyes as I asked her the question again.

"Didn't your boys tell you?" Lilly asked me as I shook my head no.

"Oh well, word is." Lilly began when Moe, Durty, and Lil Click suddenly came back and Moe told her he had it.

I gave Lilly a puzzled look as she shook her head then squeezed my hand and I let her go. I watched her as she walked out with worry on her face and Moe stood in front of me.

"Maine lil cuzz, what your girl was finna say is this. It seems the Pooh bitch got a hit out on you. Its $75K to the first nigga to body you in here and make sure you don't make it out them gates. It seems that hoe took every dime she got from the city after getting shot and a little of somebody's else money just to get you dealt with. So, you know that leaves us at war in here as of now. That nigga you was out there grilling is Ace. Ace a real killer, like hired hitman type of killer who run the bloods in here. It seems that nigga a bitch behind bars though so he ordered his lil homie B to take the contract. That means for the next day and a half you on 24-hour security. You don't walk to the door without yo butch. We on one now homies so we hopping out on them bitches and shutting shit down. We gotta eradicate this problem before it even starts. You know the brothers on go so we goo. The only problem we may have is that Ace works with Wallace. He protects that nigga so we gotta find a way to get Wallace out the picture long enough to get them bitches." Moe said and I shook my head, wishing we could kill all of those bitches.

I stood there and thought about what Moe said as my mind went a million miles a minute. There I was facing death for the thousandth time, and once again it was because of a bitch. A bitch had gotten me into every horrible fucking situation in my life. I guess that's why it suddenly occurred to me that I should use a bitch to get me out of it.

Suddenly I thought about Lilly and how she could make moves we couldn't. I told Moe not to worry about how to get Wallace out the way, just let me know when it needed to be done. He smiled and nodded when he saw me eye Lilly as she walked back past the cell.

"Bet. Then it's on." Durty said as he walked up beside me to see what me and Moe saw.

Once he saw Lilly go back into the control room where Wallace was to check the cameras he smiled knowing we had all we needed. Durty elbowed me and smiled before he turned back to finish what he was saying.

"So, as you all know the only sure way to win a war is by utilizing the element of surprise. Since these bitches plan to sneak Quatty like our G ain't real, we're going to beat em to it.

Tomorrow morning, we strike in the showers. Nobody walks out that bitch alive unless they repping this six. After that Quatty disappears, he wasn't even in on the fight, PERIOD. I got niggas on standby to take the charges should it come to that. Quatty, we need you to have Lilly ask the lil white bitch guard to switch blocks with Wallace at the last minute in the morning, right before shower time. That way he will be in F pod, leaving his lil bitch ass snitch over here in G land. That's all we need. These niggas bout to see what hell really like." Durty said as he growled then suddenly mobbed out the cell towards the showers.

All of us were on go right with him so we quickly grabbed our shit and mobbed out as Lilly ran to catch up with us. I lagged behind a little so I could talk to her and the first thing she did was ask me what was going on. I told her what I had found out and what we planned to do before I eased in the part she would play. I should have just said the shit though, because Lilly quickly agreed and asked me was that all I needed before she turned to leave.

"Damn yo bitch is a ridah." Moe said as I stood at the shower door and watched Lilly walk away.

That nigga was right too and I told him that before we dapped then went into the showers. We shit, shaved, and bathed without incident then went back to our cell following Lilly, ready just in case. Niggas wouldn't even look at us as we mobbed through that bitch like the black plague. Lilly brought around our dinner after that and we ate, smoked, then played Play Station until Moe big ass passed out.

When I was sure him and click were sleep I pulled out my burner and called Tinka for the first time since court. The phone rang a dozen times and each time my heart raced faster and faster. By the time the answering machine popped up and Tinka's voice filled my ears I was up on my feet and pacing the floor.

I called that muthafucka 50 more times as I paced before I gave up frustrated, and threw the phone on the bed. I needed to talk to Tinka and find out what was going on in her head when she knew Pooh was crazy as fuck. I wanted the opportunity to tell my side of the story but from the way shit was looking I wouldn't get that chance until I got out. If I would even get it then.

All of the shit with Tinka, Pooh and niggas in jail started to weigh heavy on me at that moment and I felt like I was about to go fucking crazy I braced myself on my bed and put my head down as I growled and tried to blow out my frustration. By the time I looked up Lilly was standing there like my little thick angel. She had the softest, most sincere look in her eyes as she stuck her hand through the bars and called me over.

"Quatty baby, come here." She said as I walked over to her with my head down and let her rest her hand on my head.

Lilly ran her fingers across my waves as she shhhed me like a baby.

"Shhh baby, it's alright. I know you got a lot you carrying right now. Do what you gotta do in here to make sure you get out king, I got you on that. I'm gonna play my part and do anything else that I can. As far as that shit with Tinka and Pooh goes." Lilly began as I suddenly looked up at her wondering how the fuck she knew anything.

"Yeah I know baby. I was in the back during your preliminary, I heard and saw it all. I also heard and saw some shit you didn't. Know that Tinka loves you baby and she's never going to leave you. Y'all child is her main concern and she's not sure how to protect the baby. I heard her talking so I know about the first baby too. She blames herself and she's afraid it will happen again. She's dealing with just as much out there as you are in here baby, so try to understand. She not gone nowhere though king so don't let that push you over the edge." Lilly said as I stood there looking confused wondering why she was cheerleading for Tinka.

I mean, for a bitch in love she sure was rooting for her rival and that threw me off. I was just about to ask her about that too when she did what Tinka always had done, and that was read my mind.

"I'm telling you this because I'm real. I know real love when I see it Quatty and I know that's what you and Tinka have. I don't want you in here thinking crazy and crashing the fuck out when I know shit that can help you. I love you too Quatty, probably just as much as Tinka. That's why I'm not ashamed to say that I also know it's possible to love two people at once and be happy. That's what I want us to have but to get there we gotta get you out. Stay focused on your goals King and let everything else work itself out. Tomorrow morning I'll do my part and you end that part of your problems. I already handled that Lay Lay bitch so hopefully Pooh gets the picture. That just leaves us and you getting Tinka to see life from a different perspective. Two wives is always better than one and that's what I want for you my king. Now, go rest your wary head handsome. I'm working a double so I'll be here when you get up." Lilly said as she kissed her hand then stuck it back through the bars to place on my lips.

"Okay baby. Goodnight my Lilly." I said just taken aback by the bad bitch I had snagged.

I fell asleep that night still a bit on edge but optimist that shit would go right. I dreamed about my life with Tinka, our baby, and Lilly as I slept and that shit felt real. It felt right. I woke up the next morning hyped and ready to go at six-thirty like planned. Lilly was there at the door like she was supposed to be and told me everything was set. She told me the lil white girl was ready and was about to go switch pods with Wallace so Ace and his crew would have no help.

I told her okay and then turned to wake up Moe and Lil Click. They jumped up, already dressed as soon as I touched them and we grabbed all our weapons and got ready. Lilly was back at our door in three minutes with Durty and eight other brothers behind her. I blew her a kiss as she giggled and winked then ran to the control room to let us out.

As soon as the bars rolled we went to work, planting butches and pipes throughout the shower. I stashed a butch made out of a piece of solid metal in my sock right before we took our places. Me and the homies posted up in place throughout the shower, just hidden out of immediate view. When Lilly walked past the door and tapped lightly three times I knew her little white friend Sarah was waking Ace's side of the pod to showers.

That was our get set moment as we all grabbed our weapons and prepared for a bloodbath. Just then Durty tapped Lil Click and told him to turn on the shower he and I was hiding in. Lil Click quickly did what Durty said and then got back in his spot, but the look on his face was classic as he wondered what the fuck Durty was doing.

"So Quatty can wash off all the blood and get the fuck out asap. Dumb muthafucka. Remind me to slap the shit out of you later." Durty said as I damn near laughed and fucked up my beast mode.

I held that shit though and good thing I did because just then front side marched in with Ace leading the line. He mobbed in that bitch with his head held high and eyes low from the loud he had smoked, oblivious to the danger that lurked. By the time all nine of them were in, the door had closed, and lil B had spotted us it was far too late.

Durty took the lead as he mobbed past me and Lil Click out of his shower stall and met lil B with a pipe to the face. I wasted no time as well jumping with the shit and coming out with butch in hand. Ace saw me coming and tried to move but my years of hooping and being the best at it gave me an advantage. I had that Mitumba reach and Allen Iverson speed as I ran up on that bitch, swerved to the side with him and reached over two niggas poking him in the left side of the neck with the butch.

When I did that blood instantly sprayed everywhere and I knew I had hit the right spot. I had poke that bitch in that main artery on my first try, a trick Lilly had put me on to. Ace, the most feared hitman in the south, was left standing there holding the hole in his fucking neck and bleeding out. The nigga most fools fear had been taken out by a young, hooping, college nigga turned goon. It was like when David slayed Goliath with that damn rock as I watched Ace stumble back and his homies yell his name.

I laughed my evil, Durty laugh at them bitches as I glanced around and saw my niggas boding bitches everywhere. I didn't have time to gloat though because before I could even wipe the blood off my face, one of the niggas I had reached over came at me with a butch. I stood back with my long legs and kicked that bitch in the chest as soon as he got close. That nigga wasn't expecting that shit so he flew back like a fucking ragdoll and I was on his ass.

I wasn't even trying to fight them niggas at that point, especially not when they had come to kill me. All I wanted to do was eliminate all threats in between me and my freedom, and at that moment he was one. That's why I gave that bitch a buck fifty across the face as he flapped around like a fish. Two solid rights and three pokes to the chest later, I got up off that bitch covered in blood just as Lilly ran into the bathroom.

"What the fuck?" She yelled after she stepped in and saw blood and bodies everywhere.

I glanced around to see what she saw and when I did my stomach turned. A piece of an ear lay right by my foot and fingers and shit were scattered everywhere. All of my niggas were covered in blood too like some shit off a horror movie. I think I went into slight shock after that shit because the next thing I knew I was back in my cell, wet, and Lil Click was telling me to put my shirt on.

"Put yo shirt on bruh. They'll be calling riot squad in a minute. We been in our cell all morning though, still locked down." Click said as I looked at the door and saw that Lilly had rolled our bars.

I sat there in a dazed state as Click rambled about the fight and Moe sat quietly cleaning the blood off his shoes. I didn't hear shit Click said or anything for that matter until Moe suddenly called my name.

"Quatty, you aite cuzz? You look lost as fuck over there." Moe said as he stood up and walked over to me.

"Nah bruh. What the fuck happened? Last thing I saw was Lilly walk in." I said still kinda dazed and confused as fuck.

I stood up to put on my shirt as Moe looked at Lil Click then turned to look back at me.

"Yeah lil cuzz, you in shock. Sit back down for a minute." Moe said as I did just that and he sat down beside me to tell me what happened.

"Maine bruh after Lilly came in shit really went bad. One of them niggas grabbed her up and poked her in the shoulder. That was his fuck up though cause after that nigga you went muthafucking crazy. I can guarantee they will be picking pieces of that bitch out of the shower drain for weeks. We had to drag you off him fool and to the showers. After that yo ass was moving like a robot and not saying shit. I knew what was going on though. The same thing happened to me the first time I saw a massacre. That's why we had Lilly dress you before I fixed up her shoulder, and you been sitting here ever since. The shit over though fool cause Lilly handled that. She got us back in here and locked down before the other side came out and then they discovered the bodies, supposedly. C.O.'s think it was a beef between Ace nem and the other part so for right now we good. You good though cuzz?" Moe asked me as I soaked in everything he said.

Hearing what had happened was what I needed to snap out of whatever the fuck I was in. In seconds I was up on my feet and at the bars looking for Lilly.

"I knew it was something bad fool cause I ain't blacked out like that since I was a young nigga. Where Lilly at though? She aite? Aye yo C.O." I yelled as I hung on the bars and C.O's walked past without even looking at me.

"She aite bruh. She in a meeting about what happened. Let's just chill and wait this shit out." Moe said and I agreed before I sat down.

We sat and talked for about thirty minutes as I kept my eyes open, searching the pod for Lilly. When I saw her come out of the office with Wallace and two others and shake her head I knew something was up.

"Something up bruh. Watch Lilly for me." I said to Moe just as Lilly walked out of the pod with another officer and Wallace came straight to me.

He stopped right in front of the bars and stared at me before he signaled for them to open the gate while I folded my arms and exchanged his glare.

"Turn around and put your hands behind your back Jones. You're going to the hole." Wallace said as I told him he had me fucked up because I hadn't done anything.

I guess his big weak ass could tell I wasn't playing by the look in my eyes because he didn't say shit back. He just signaled for the other officers in the control room to come out and help him.

"Now we can do this the easy way Jones or the hard way. It's your decision. Either way it goes though bitch, you going to the hole. I know you had something to do with this shit and until I find out bitch you gonna be in a hole by yourself. You better hope you get out tomorrow. If you resist this shit I know you won't though because you'll be in Sick Bay. So, what's it gonna be BITCH?" Wallace asked as I balled up my fists ready to pop off.

I knew I had a good plan to get him but at that moment I would risk it all just to break that bitch nigga's face. I was about to do it too but Moe stopped me just in time. He grabbed my hand and when I turned to look at him he shook his head no. I respected that because I knew my big homie knew jail better than I did. That's why I decided not to hit that bitch but I still wasn't willing to just go to the hole when he couldn't tell me what I did.

"Maine what did I do to go to the fucking hole. I didn't do shit. I been locked down all night right here with everybody else. Why the fuck you come to me? Cause you don't fucking like me nigga?" I yelled as the white officer with Wallace told him he was wrong and said that I hadn't done anything.

"I don't give a fuck if YOU think he didn't do shit. This lil bitch always doing something." Wallace yelled to the officer before he turned back to me.

"Yes, it's because I don't like you lil bitch. That's all the reason I need. Now bring yo hoe ass on or I'll spray yo ass." Wallace said as he pulled out his pepper spray and I told that bitch to do it.

We stood there and stared at each other for a minute as I dared that bitch to do it with my eyes. Just when I was getting tired of waiting and was about to punch him and get shit popping, his fat ass sprayed me and it was on. I got one good, solid punch to that bitch's nose before they all jumped on me, but I still bucked them bitches until the end. They brought me out that hoe screaming and fighting as that white C.O., Baker, continued to tell Wallace he was wrong.

I could still hear them arguing about it after Wallace threw me into the tiny, nasty ass cell with nothing but a toilet and sink combo, and blanket to keep me company. I could tell Wallace was going to be in deep shit behind it too after Baker said he was reporting him. That shit made me so happy I couldn't help but to laugh as I stood up and put my face on the screen in the door.

"Ahhh big bitch. Now, you see what snitching hoes get. Just wait though sucker. Yo hell just begun. Bitch ass." I said to Wallace before Baker told him to come out and they turned and left.

I'm sure his bitch ass heard me laughing all the way back to the pod because I laughed so fucking hard I fell on to the floor.

I laid there the rest of the night thinking about all I had done and been through. I remembered how all my hell had begun and wished I could turn back the hands of time. I stared at the bruises and cuts on my knuckles from the faces I crushed and told myself that was not who I really was.

I told myself I was better than that and that I could leave all of that bullshit behind me when I walked out of those doors. That's the shit I told myself but I wasn't too sure I really believed it. That beast that lived inside of me was always ready and on go, I just hoped that once I was out I would be able to tame him again. I knew I needed to especially if I wanted a life with Tinka our baby, and Lilly too. I knew I had to get all of that killer shit out of my system so that I could focus on what really mattered.

"Tomorrow is the last day I show the beast unless it's necessary, I just need this one last chance to destroy the evil that had tried to destroy me. I'm ready for this one last dance." I said out loud to myself right before I closed my eyes.

# Chapter 8

Baker woke me up the next morning after the massacre, my release day, at about four with fresh, street clothes in hand and an apologetic expression on his face. I could tell from that look that he wore that he had done what he does best, and that's snitch. That along with the fact that he was the one letting me out of the hole and not Wallace, let me know his fat at ass had gotten in trouble and removed from my pod roster. That made me happy as hell so I floated out of that bitch and pass Baker as he apologized and cuffed my wrists.

"Jones, me and the department want to apologize for the actions of Officer Wallace. He was totally out of line and if you would like to file formal charges I would be happy to take you to complete the process right now. That's why I came to get you so early. Well, that and the fact you didn't deserve to be here anyway. Wallace overstepped his power because of personal feelings and accused and punished an innocent person. We found those responsible so you are totally cleared. I will take you to file the complaint now, then back to your pod for your goodbyes and breakfast, then at 6:45 promptly I will be back to take you to process you out." Baker said as I nodded then we walked out of the containment unit.

I turned and looked back one last time before I followed Baker to file the complaint. I never wanted to see that rotten fucking place again, and I damn sure was going to work hard to stay away. That meant staying focused on living and protecting my family. That meant providing for my family and eliminating any threats that could hinder their happiness. Wallace was one of those threats. That's why I marched with my head high to the office with Baker to file that complaint. Although I was not down with snitching, I made an exception of the rule in his case.

I wanted that fat hoe to have so much shit on his head that, once they came and got him and locked his ass up, he would never see daylight again. That's the bullshit he wished on me and that was the fate I was going to ensure he had. I filed that fucking complaint like a white lady snitching in the movies because someone was talking too loud and eating food they brought from home.

When I was done, the personnel rep apologized just like Baker did and told me the issue would be handled. I could tell from that tight, school teacher ass bun, witch face, and thick cat woman glasses that she wore, she meant business so I knew Wallace big, black ass had hell to pay. That added with the laundering scheme and the finale I had planned was the sweet revenge I needed so I felt like a million bucks as I strolled back into the pod and that bitch came to life.

Everybody in that bitch were on their feet cheering and shit as I came in. Niggas who didn't even fuck with me, niggas on rival teams even stood up and showed love because they respected the way I moved. I ain't gonna lie, that shit felt good, but at the same time it hurt. It hurt me to go from a nigga who was adored and loved for his talent, intelligence and looks. To a nigga feared and respected because of his ability to be brutal, deadly, and cut throat.

That's not what I wanted to teach my seed. I had vowed whenever I had kids to be the best man I could be to lead by example. That was not the example I was talking about. That's why I planned to shed that shit like bad skin the moment I walked out those doors, and never look back.

That was how I was going to find peace. I knew that and I was, but I had to celebrate and handle business first.

I walked into the cell I shared with Moe and Lil Click and they both turned the fuck up along with Durty.

"QUATTYYYYYY! YOU OUT THIS BITCH! YOU A FREE MAN NIGGA! QUATTYYYY!!!" They yelled as they showed me love and handed me blunts they had lit.

We smoked and tripped for a while as I gave away every fucking thing I had and thought about what I would do first as soon as I was free. As I thought I got dressed in the fresh ass True Religion set Lilly had brought me while I daydreamed about a hot and steamy threesome with Tinka and Lilly and my niggas talked shit. Lilly broke my haze when she appeared at the bars and told me it was on.

"All systems go baby. Baker is on his way to get you and Wallace is on his way to the little boy's cell right now. By the time they walk you out of processing he should be caught and on his way in as you come out. Big punk bitch. He tried to get me fired for the shit yesterday. Nigga don't know I'm smarter than the average bitch. I added three more charges to his big ass. Soon king…its US!" Lilly said before she blew me a kiss and disappeared into the pod.

Just like planned, Baker was at the bars ten minutes later ready to take me to freedom. I said my goodbyes to Lil Click and Durty and gave Durty the information on where he could find me when he got out in two weeks. After that, I turned back to Moe as he stood by the bars with a small slip of paper in his hands and tears in his eyes. It was hard as fuck for me to leave my big cousin behind just like it was hard for him to see me go, but there wasn't shit I could do because he was in that bitch for life.

"Damn lil cousin. I'm glad you getting out of this hell hole nigga but I sholl hate to see you go. Stay up out there nigga and stay the fuck out the way. Here." Moe said after he hugged me and handed me the piece of paper her had in his hand.

"This is the address to a house I own down in Charlotte, North Carolina. It's yours. I got some money, the deed to the house, and instructions in a P.O. Box at the post office by the house. Go there and get that shit. AND LIVE HAPPILY EVER AFTER NIGGA…for all of us!" Moe said as I sucked up the tears that threatened to fall before I gave him dap.

I walked out that bitch feeling conflicted, hating to leave my homies behind but anxious to be free. I stopped at the door to the pod to look at Moe and Lil Click one last time as niggas cheered and showed me love.

"AITE, I'M OUT. YALL NIGGAS STAY UP. AND GIVE THE DEVIL HELL WHEN HE GET IN THIS BITCH.74 TIL THE WORLD BLOW. GD!!!" I yelled as all of my brothers yelled back and Baker led me out of the pod.

I felt nervous like a welfare recipient on their way to a drug test as I was processed out and received the belongings I came in with. I was so nervous to be free again I almost did know how to get out the bitch, the lady had to point me in the right direction.

"One more step and you're out of here. And look at your parting gift." Lilly whispered from behind me after I walked out of processing and back into the back hall.

I turned and smiled at her before I turned to look at what she was focused on and what I saw was the best shit ever. There was Wallace being drug away from F pod with his pants half way down, blood on his head, and cuffs on his muthafucking wrists. Wallace looked like he had tried to fight and they whooped his ass because there were bumps and bruises all over his big ass. The little white boy was being led away behind him with a blanket around him and two nurses holding him up. He looked up and smiled at me as I nodded my head telling him he had done good.

I made a mental note to call Moe as soon as I was settled to have him give the white boy the G I promised him for helping me take down Wallace, as they led his big ass right by me. He tried his best not to look my way but I made sure that bitch saw me as I stepped in front of them.

"Haaaa. Ole Wallace. Look at you now." I said as I laughed and he looked off to the side.

"Have fun in hell pussy. I know you like the top but I think that for the next 60 years of your life it will be the life of a bottom. I hope they fuck the lining out of your big rotten ass." I whispered as Wallace finally looked at me and saw the joy in my eyes as I saw the fear and misery in his.

"Welcome to hell pussy. My niggas got you a welcome home present waiting. Good luck bitch!" I said before I walked away laughing at Wallace punk ass.

That was all I needed to leave jail better than I had come in. At the door, Baker told me bye and allowed Lilly to walk me out. We waited on him to leave the port before she turned to me and smiled.

"So, this is it huh king? This is our last moment together in this place. I hope it won't be our last moment forever." Lilly said as I reached over and quickly rubbed her face.

I wanted to kiss her fine ass and whisk her up in my arms like on the corny ass movies, but I knew we were under surveillance. Instead I just winked my eye at her and blew a kiss, and she caught it in the ar.

"You ain't getting rid of me that easily girl, this is just the beginning. See you soon my beautiful queen. Love you Lilly." I said quickly before I opened the door and walked out to freedom.

I looked back at the gate and saw Lilly as she stood there with a tear in her eye. She yelled out that she loved me too before I walked out of the gate and to the life of a free man. As soon as I made it to the other side I took out running like a track star at the Olympics. It felt good as fuck to have the sun on my back and wind on my skin as I ran towards the parking lot. As soon as I got there I stopped dead in my tracks as Tinka, Ghost, and Belle stood on the car waiting. I wasted no time as I ran to my queen and wrapped her in my arms.

"Tinka. Tinka baby, you're here. I love you and I'm so sorry baby." I babbled as I hugged her tightly and she held me tighter while she cried in my arms.

"I love you too my king. I love you more than life." Tinka said and I dropped some tears knowing all I had done and had to tell her.

I wasn't about to do that shit then though, not when everything was finally good. I decided to tell her on the ride home as I kissed all over her face.

"Aite that's enough of that shit. Let us get some love too." Ghost finally said and me and Tinka laughed.

I let Tinka go and shook my nigga up then hugged Belle before I turned to look back at the jail.

"I never want to see this muthafucka again. Let's get the fuck away from here." I said after a few seconds and Tinka agreed.

I grabbed her hand before I kissed her juicy lips and prepared to ride away in the sunset. Just as we turned to get into my truck which Tinka had drove to get me, a white Maximum pulled up in front of us and a beaten up Lay Lay jumped out.

"Quatty you punk muthafucka, sending that bitch to fight me. You better be glad Pooh still love yo ass our I would body you right here at the jail." The bitch yelled as she went over to open the passenger door so Pooh could talk.

I told Tinka to get into the truck as I walked a little closer and Ghost walked over with me.

"Maine, get y'all maggot asses on. Ole nasty, worthless ass bitches. You hoes tried to have me killed but that shit didn't work. Just get the fuck on before I catch another muthafucking charge." I said as Pooh cried and told me I was a liar.

"Come on now Quatty. What you mean? You lied to me. You said if I told them that story and you got out we could get back together. What about that? Did you tell your bitch that? Did you tell her you said you still love me and that she not worth it? Huh? Did you Quatty? Talk to me." Pooh yelled from the passenger seat like a lunatic as me and Ghost laughed at her ass.

I had no sympathy for that bitch or her feelings.

"Bitch, a nigga will say any muthafucking thing in a crunch. You served your purpose ole maggot ass hoe. Now kick rocks. I'm done with you bitch. And guess what, I'm getting married. Now I won hoe so be gone foe I call the police out here to get yo hot ass." I said to Pooh as I laughed and she cried while Ghost repeated what I said.

When I was done talking I gave my nigga some dap then we got in our cars as some officers walked out. That was enough to scare them maggots away so Lay Lay quickly closed Pooh's door before she ran around to jump back in the driver's seat.

"This shit ain't over Quatty. It ain't over. I'm on yo ass till the death of me." Pooh yelled as Lay Lay sped off and I laughed at her ass.

"If that's what she wants, so be it." Tinka said as I pulled off and told her it was done.

As soon as I pulled out of the parking lot and onto the main road I felt like old Quatty again. No more did I have to watch my back and fight like an animal to survive. I felt like a new man as I pushed 80 in my Cadillac truck and Tinka reached over to grab my hand. Her touch felt so fucking good, I wanted to pull over and dick her down right there. Big stomach and all.

I looked over at her and smiled as I saw all the love and loyalty I deserved in her eyes. That was enough to bring my guilty conscious to life and I suddenly spilled my fucking guts.

"Baby, you know I love you right?" I began and Tinka looked at me like I was crazy.

I could tell that she knew I was about to make a confession because I started off the same way she did when she told me she had set me up. I peeked at her out of the corner of my eye as she leaned forward and turned the radio down. My fucking heart beat in my throat as she burned a hole in the side of my face with her eyes and I tried to find the right words to say.

"Just tell me baby. You know you can tell me anything and we will work through it." Tinka said as I swallowed down the lump in my throat while I seriously doubted what she had said.

I doubted she would be that easy to forgive when she actually found out what I had to tell. I glanced over and saw the tears in her eyes before I proceeded to tell the truth.

"Well baby, Pooh wasn't lying I did tell her all that shit. I told her what I had to in order to get out and I'm sorry for not saying anything." I said as Tinka deeply exhaled then began to laugh.

I had to look over at her ass crazy after that because I couldn't understand why she was laughing.

"Wasup baby? Why you laughing?" I asked Tinka.

"Because I already knew that Quatty. I'm not that stupid." Tinka said and I shook my head because I knew that she wasn't.

I knew that my chick was smarter than the average and up on game too. I had to smile at her beautiful ass as she sat there and acted like she was waiting on me to tell her something else. I did actually have another confession about Lilly, but there was no way she knew about that, or so I thought.

"I also know about Lilly." Tinka suddenly said and I damn near lost control of the truck.

I had to pull that bitch over into a Krystal's parking lot after that so I could turn and look at Tinka's ole detective ass. As soon as I had parked and turned the truck off I did just that and Tinka laughed again.

"Why you looking so astonished Quatty? I knew about her since our first visit. You think I don't know game and how jail works, everybody need a bitch behind bars. I knew somebody was moving your work inside the jail and when I saw her lil thick ass I knew she was your type. So, tell me. How deep is the relationship? Was it just jail or you plan on seeing her now that you're out? Just know that I'm fine either way as long as I have you." Tinka said casually like it wasn't shit, and I thought I was hearing things.

I couldn't believe I had found two loyal, fine females who were willing to share me and my love. I felt like I had won the fucking lottery on my way home from robbing a weed dispensary. I was so happy I didn't even respond before I leaned over and kissed Tinka with so much passion her eyes crossed. That answered her question for her, but when I let her go I still felt the need to explain the situation.

"Baby, I love you and I want nothing more than to be with you for the rest of my life. But I won't lie, I got feelings for Lilly too. She held me down when you couldn't and showed me she really cares for a nigga. As a matter of fact, she cares about us both and the baby. She wants to be a family with us and I think I want that too. What you feel about it though because I don't want shit you don't want. I'll walk away from her and everything else if you say so Nicole." I said to Tinka as I saw her eyes soften and a tear ran down her cheek. I held my breath as she sat there silently and stared into my eyes. I just knew she was about to tell me that we were done when she opened her mouth. However, what she said shocked me.

"I want what you want Quatty. I want you to be happy. You don't know this but I was raised in a polygamous family, my mama just didn't know it for about eight years. However, when she found out she gave my dad an ultimatum, either bring her home and we all live together or she would walk away and he could be with only her. After that, my house was happy again with mama, daddy, and aunt Tera, raising and providing for us. I think that the situation can definitely work if everyone is on the same page. I've talked to her a few times when I visited and she was always extra nice and professional. I caught her looking at my ass a couple of times too so I knew she got down with the carpet munching." Tinka said laughing and lightened the mood enough that I laughed too.

"Yeah but on the real baby, I'm cool with it. I think she fine as hell too, and if you trust her with your life in there I know we can trust her out here. So, I guess what I'm saying is… when she coming home?" Tinka asked me and I sat there looking stupid not knowing what to say.

There I was with everything I ever wanted within reach and I couldn't even find the words to say. I had to take in a few breaths and pinch my fucking self to make sure that shit was real. It was so I hugged Tinka again and kissed her lips passionately.

"I don't know about coming home but I'll invite her over tomorrow so we can get to know each other. She has a 5-year-old son name Damion too so you will have an instant son. This shit might really work out. I guess, we will see. We gotta get our shit straight first. My cousin, Big Moe, gave me this address and shit." I said as I pulled the slip of paper Moe had given me out of my pocket and handed it to Tinka.

"The nigga said it's the address to a mini mansion he bought before he got sentenced to life and the key to a P.O. Box full of money will be waiting. We can leave and start the fuck over." I said with excitement in my voice that seeped into Tinka.

I watched her perk up before my eyes as she sat up straight in her chair and pulled out her phone to look up the address. I gave her the address and in seconds she was squealing and bouncing in her seat.

"Ahhhhh. Hell yeah, this house big as fuck and it's in a nice neighborhood. Can we leave tonight?" Tinka said as I laughed and told her no, but we could leave by Saturday.

"Let's just stay for this week, wrap up loose ends, and see if we want to take Lilly with us. Then after that, we out of this bitch and we ain't never looking back." I said as I kissed Tinka again then crunk up and left the parking lot.

"Yes we are big daddy, witcho lucky ass. Yo girl got a girlfriend!" Tinka said as she laughed so hard the baby started doing flips in her stomach and she yelled out in pain.

I reached over and grabbed her stomach as she moaned and laughed while the baby moved. For the first time, I felt the life I had helped to create and that shit made me cry. I rode all the way to the house Tinka had gotten in Millington with my hand on her stomach and those same tears in my eyes. By the time we pulled into the driveway Tinka's pain had subsided and she looked excited as hell.

"We're hereeee. Come on baby. Get out." Tinka squealed as I suddenly looked around and saw all of the cars lined up and down the street.

I looked at Tinka crazy as she hopped her little round belly ass out and wobbled around to my door as I locked it.

"Come on Quatty. Stop playing. Get out of the car maine." Tinka said laughing as she pulled on the door handle and I shook my head no.

I knew exactly what was going on from the cars and I wanted no parts of the surprise, welcome home party she had planned. I had my mind set on a long, hot bath, a good meal, and then some pussy for dessert. I didn't feel like being festive. Hell, all I wanted to do after six, almost seven months was to get freaky. It was written on my face too as I bit my lip, but continued to shake my head saying no to Tinka.

"Nope little Umpa Lumpa. Get away from my car girl. I know this some type of welcome home party and I want no parts of it. All I want to do is shit, shave, bathe, and then have a quiet dinner and you for dessert. A party? Hell nah, ain't nobody got time for that shit so gwon. Gwon girl." I said from behind the glass as Tinka laughed her ass off.

I loved to see her smile, looking all beautiful and shit without a care in the world. That's how I wanted every moment of our lives to be and I was determined to get us there.

"Come on Quatty, I promise it will be fast. Two hours at the most. I already told their asses we needed some alone time so they couldn't stay. Belle and Ghost got their own side of the house so we ain't gotta worry about them. Just get out of the car, put on your happy face, and we can get through this quickly. Then we can get to the freaky shit and gone work this baby out. I'm nine months today so it's safe to say that a couple long strokes from daddy dick will do the trick. Soooo, come on Mandingo so I can fuck yo lights out." Tinka said before she licked out that long, thick, juicy ass tongue she had and my dick got hard.

I jumped out that bitch so fast she had to jump back so I wouldn't hit her with the door.

"Come on dammit. Why you still standing here. We gotta go party in fast forward so they can get the hell out our house. Come on with your beautiful, pregnant ass." I said jokingly as Tinka laughed her ass off and I led her into the house by her hand.

As soon as we got inside everyone jumped out like they were really surprising me and the party was on.

"My muthafucking nigga!!!" Peedy yelled as he and Ghost wrapped me up in a bear hug by the door.

"Let me go while y'all being gay. My stomach can't take bromance." Tinka said joking as she grabbed her stomach while walking away.

We all laughed as we let go of our embrace and my niggas shook me up.

"Maine fool, it's so good to see you. The muthafucking crew back together again. So tell me nigga, is that max shit really like OZ with niggas getting shanked and raped and shit." Peedy asked as Ghost asked him was he on drugs and I laughed at their dumb asses.

I told Peedy to find us all a corner to smoke and talk in so that I could mingle with everybody else first, then I went off to speak. I must have hugged and talked to fifty people as I searched facing, looking for two of the most important women in my world. It took me a while but I found them in the kitchen hooking it up

"Ummm, damn it smells good in here. Is that the best mama and the most beautiful sister in the world in here making me the fyest meal ever." I said as I snuck in behind them and they turned around shocked as hell.

"Quatty, my baby." My mama said as she wrapped me in her arms and tears fell down her face.

My sister wrapped her arms around us both and we stood there for a while and hugged as my mama cried and prayed.

"Thank you Lord for bringing my son home in one peace and allowing him to have a second chance." My mama said as I said Amen and we all left the embrace.

"What y'all got going in here though? I smell lasagna, greens, and some more." I said as I opened a pot of greens cooking on the stove and the aroma made me weak.

"Get out of my pot Quatty. It ain't time yet. Get in there and enjoy yo party and I'll call you when it's ready." My mama said as she popped my hand and I dropped the second fork of greens I was trying to eat.

I pushed my sister and she yelled to my mother as I danced towards the door.

"Oh yeah mama. I'll be ready to eat after I go duck off with the boys. Don't let Bonnie eat all the lasagna. Or should I call you cheeseburger." I said calling my sister the childhood nickname she hated and she threw a towel at me as I ran out.

I felt like my old self again as I ran away laughing, free to be myself and not the beast. I found Ghost and Peedy in the garage engrossed in a deep conversation about hoes and rollin blunts. I walked in just as Peedy said no hoe would ever willingly share her man with another bitch.

"Oh, I beg to differ Professor Gangsta because I got two of those women myself." I said as I came in and both of them turned around laughing.

I sat down with my niggas on the futon in the garage and filled them in on everything that happened in jail. By the time I finished telling them about the arrangement between me, Tinka, and Lilly, both of them were on their knees hailing me like a king.

"All hail pussy King Quatty. The first hood nigga EVER with two wives." Peedy said as Ghost joined in and I laughed at their asses.

We all sat there and smoked and chilled, talking about how good my life was going to be until my mama called us to eat. After that we had a great dinner with everyone in the living room and dining room eating and catching up. After dinner, we had another smoke session then the crowd started to thin out. By four that evening the last people had left, which was my mama and sister, and me, Tinka, Ghost, and Belle were left alone in the house.

"Where the kids at?" I asked Belle as we all sat on the huge sectional.

"Them little spoiled bastards in Atlanta until Wednesday so you know what time it is." Belle said as she looked at Ghost and he smirked and jumped up.

"Well, Uhhhh." Ghost said yawning and stretching before he grabbed Belle's hand and pulled her to her feet.

"I'm tired as hell so I guess we'll go to sleep. Or freak." Ghost said and we all laughed as he pulled Belle out the room and she fake cried.

Me and Tink sat there and laughed for a minute then she suddenly looked at me.

"I want a little nasty time too Big Daddy, so bring that big dick on." Tinka said as she got up and grabbed my hand too.

She didn't have to ask me twice because the next thing she knew I was whisking her pregnant but not heavy ass up in my arms and carrying her to our bedroom. I put her down as soon as we got through the door and stood there looking at all the pictures she had on the wall. Over the months, we had been together before I went to jail, Tinka had photographed everything. She had pics of us lying in bed, out at the mall, and even at church, hanging on the wall.

"I had to keep you near me King, now I want you inside of me. Give me one second then I want you to get naked." Tinka said before she kissed me then wobbled into the master bath.

I lingered behind and finished looking at the pictures everywhere, remembering how our love affair began. I hated that we got together under false pretenses but I wouldn't trade our love for anything. I stood there and looked into Tinka's beautiful eyes in a pic of us at the mall. I hoped that I could keep that type of light in her eyes when it was more than her to share my love.

She broke my thoughts when she yelled my name and told me to get naked and in the bathroom. Before she could get room out her mouth I was already ass naked and stepping into the water. My baby welcomed me with open arms and washed my body like I was on Coming to America and then I returned the favor. When we got out, I dried her body then carried her off to bed. I looked into her eyes as I walked and said everything in my heart without uttering a word. I laid her down on the bed and she looked up at me with those bedroom eyes as my manhood stood up stiff.

"I love you Nicole." I said as she said she loved me too and I hovered above her to kiss her lips.

I kissed her and then made my way down her neck; licking, kissing, and sucking everything I passed. I put her breasts in my mouth one by one and sucked them like a nursing baby. She moaned in delight and grinded her hips as I made my way over her belly straight to her honeypot. When I got there, I was so excited I had to stop and admire its beauty first.

Once that was out of my system, I opened Tinka's lips like a flower then slurped and kissed that big, pink pussy until her clit was swollen. I ate that shit like a porn star and made Tinka shake like a leaf on a tree. About ten minutes after my oral assault began Tinka was shaking uncontrollably as I drank down her juices until the last drop. I sucked and licked until her organism was gone and she was hot and ready again. I felt my dick growing as Tinka moaned and I wondered how we would do it with her belly so big. As usual, she knew my thoughts so as I kissed back up her body she grabbed my chin to hold my face up.

"Don't be scared baby, we can do this safely you just can't be on top. Now bring that dick here." Tinka said as she turned on her side and I got in the pussy from behind.

Mane, when I stuck my dick inside of her creamy, warm, wetness I thought I would nut off the muscle. I held my shit together though as I slowed down my stroke and focused on pleasing her and not myself. I slow grinded Tinka from the side as I kissed her neck and whispered in her ear.

"I love you baby. Forever." I panted as Tinka moaned and said she loved me too.

She grinded her hips, tightened her walls, and threw that pussy back at me like a pro and for a second I forgot she was pregnant. Before I knew it, I had grabbed her hair and began to drill that little pink starburst. She screamed and bit the covers as I went to work while licking her neck in that special spot. Soon neither one of us could take it and we bust together and fell into a puddle of our own sweat. I was lost in euphoria as I laid there beside the love of my life, spent and happy as hell. Tinka had given me some welcome home pussy I would never forget.

"I love you baby and I can't wait for us to spend the rest of our lives together; me, you, and Lilly. Now call her and tell her to come and spend a night." Tinka said as she suddenly reached over, grabbed her phone off the nightstand and handed it to me.

I looked at her crazy as she bucked her eyes and told me to stop being a punk.

"Punk? Punk? Not me. Don't you know my name Quatty girl. I ain't never been a punk." I said as Tinka laughed and laid her head on my chest.

"Okay Quatty, get yo shaky ass on the phone and call our girl then. I'm gonna take a nap until she gets here." Tinka said and I kissed her forehead before she closed her eyes.

I laid there for a minute with the phone in hand and Tinka on my chest as thought about how different my life was becoming. I smiled to myself as I saw happiness in my future just beyond the darkness. I wanted that life that lie ahead all I had to do was get Tinka and Lilly together to make sure they were compatible, thereby securing my forever threesome. Most importantly though, I had to make it through one week in Memphis.

That sounded like an easy enough task but one week on the streets of Memphis was just as dangerous as a month in jail. That's why I planned on playing it safe with Pooh on the warpath. I was going to lay low, make sure shit was in order for the move, then get the fuck away. I just had to get Lilly on board too. I had to make that phone call and get shit started.

"Hello, wassup baby? You ready to come home?" I said to Lilly after I dialed the number and she answered on the first ring.

That was the beginning of the best times in my life. The quiet before the storm!

# Chapter 9

I talked to Lilly on the phone that evening for about twenty minutes, just chopping it up about real life and not all that jailhouse shit. Lilly showed real interest in my life and being a part of it as she asked me about my welcome home party. I told her it was lit and how we wished she could have come, but it wasn't too late.

"Oh really now? Is that you inviting me or the both of you? How does Tinka feel about this?" Lilly said as I laughed and then kissed Tinka on her forehead to wake her up.

"I'll let you ask her that yourself." I said to Lilly as Tinka looked up at me and I kissed her lips, handed her the phone, and told her it was Lilly before I laid back on my pillow.

"Hello, is this my wife in law?" Tinka said in a soft, groggy tone as she laughed and I heard Lilly laugh through the phone too.

I couldn't help but to laugh too seeing them hit it off and I continued to smile as they held a full thirty-minute conversation then hung up. In that thirty minutes they discussed their wants, needs and desires, only stopping briefly to ask for my input. I laid there and listened as Lilly told Tinka she had cooked and was on her way over to spend the night with food because her niece was there to watch Damion.

"Sooo get ready baby. Our Lilly on the way. I like her. And, I love you! Tinka said before she kissed me again and I smiled like a Siamese cat.

I pushed her from behind as she tried to get up and then laid back to watch her wobble into the bathroom. At the door she stopped to turn and look at me and I swear that girl had a glow. She was so beautiful all radiant and full of life. I loved her more at that moment than I ever had. She was carrying my baby and about to be my wife, not to mention, allowing me to have another wife too. Tinka was like a fucking unicorn in my eyes at that moment; beautiful, majestic, and hard to find. I was glad I had her too and I was willing to do anything to keep her and our Lilly happy.

"Our Lilly." I said out loud to myself as I got up and grabbed some joggers and gray sweats before I joined Tinka in the shower.

We bathed together as we talked about the baby we were about to have and Tinka told me she never found out the gender. She said after I left, she didn't want to find out alone so she told them no so we could find out together when it came. I was happy she had said that too because I really wanted to be there every step of the way and she knew it.

"I just couldn't do it without you." Tinka said as she dried me off then kissed me on the chest.

"Besides, I don't know if it's one gender anyway. The way this little wild person be acting up, it may be two. OR THREE!" Tinka said laughing as I bucked my eyes and pretended to have a heart attack.

I laid there on the floor and played dead as Tinka dressed and walked over me. I knew she was playing but that shit took the wind out of me thinking about three babies at once. I laid there for a minute before I got up and joined Tinka, Belle, and Ghost in the living room. By then his ole high ass was hungry and he made sure we all knew it.

"Maine, a nigga about to die. Ain't no more food left? I know them folks didn't eat everything, I'm starving. Damn Belle, get yo thick ass in there and go rattle some pots." Ghost said as he slapped Belle's thigh and she slapped him across the chest.

Tinka and I laughed as we watched them get caught up in a wrestling match before we told them Lilly was bringing dinner. We had to go through the whole story of who Lilly was for Belle and when we were done I was surprised by her response just like I was with Tinka.

"Okay so where she at? I'm hungry too? She got a sister or something because I need a wife-in-law too. I get tired of this smart mouth bastard I need a hoe I can trust to take him off my hand sometimes." Belle said laughing as Ghost agreed while handing Tinka his phone.

"Call her now and tell her to bring her sister with her." Ghost said as Belle knocked his phone out of his hand and onto the floor while the doorbell rung.

"See it's too late now, she here. You missed your chance to be a sister wife girl." Ghost said as he picked up his phone and Belle popped him again while I got up to answer the door.

When I opened that muthafucka I felt like I was in a movie as Lilly smiled at me with her big brown eyes before she got on her tiptoes and kissed my lips. It was like the air stopped moving outside but only surrounded us as I got mesmerized by seeing and feeling Lilly as a free man.

"Hello my king, I'm home at last!" Lilly said as she walked past me into the house with two big bags of food in her hand.

The delicious aroma of the food and the seductive scent of her perfume made my dick hard as I stood in the door and watched her walk down the hall and straight into Tinka.

"Ohh is that my sexy Lilly, with food. Girl, you already know the way to my heart. Come on daddy so we can eat." Tinka said as she and Lilly exchanged kisses on the cheek before she took a bag out of her hand and walked into the kitchen.

"Yeah, come on daddy." Lilly said as she winked then turned to walk into the kitchen behind Tinka.

I stood there still stuck, sure that I was in a fucking dream. Belle broke my haze when she walked by smiling and shaking her head and Ghost ran up behind her.

"Ain't gotta call me twice. That shit smell good. Quatty bring yo ole Superfly looking ass on." Ghost said as he waited on me at the kitchen door and I finally closed the front door.

I walked over to him and we showed each other love as I whispered to him how the shit was a dream.

"Yeah, to lame niggas, but nigga this yo real life. Enjoy this shit homie, hell you been through enough. Now let's go fuck some up." Ghost said as we joined the ladies in the kitchen and threw down on the lasagna, steaks, loaded baked potatoes, alfredo, and Caesar salad Lilly had brought.

Everybody found out really quickly that Lilly was way more than a pretty face, fat ass, and diabolical mind. Just like Tinka, my bitch was bad. She could cook, clean, and suck a mean dick. By the time dinner was over I sat back in my chair with my hands behind my head and a full as stomach and I watched my ladies chatter like they had known each other forever. Ghost and I exchanged glances over the table before he announced that we were going to smoke.

"Go on and get high then niggas, we gonna clean then go watch a movie." Tinka said as she got up to start clearing the table and Lilly got up to help her.

"Yeah get the fuck out weed heads, but save me some. And save some energy too Ghost. Because you'll need it." Belle said laughing as my ladies joined in.

"Hell, Quatty will too." Tinka said before she looked at Lilly and they both looked at me.

For a second my damn heart raced when I thought about how fire they were separate. I couldn't imagine what I would do when I had both of them at my disposal. That fear only lasted a second though because my real nigga kicked in and told me I would make due or at least die trying.

"Y'all lil thick asses better be ready. We working with monsters over here." I said as I laughed and left the kitchen.

"Hell yeah. Mandingos, you wenches now clean them dishes." Ghost yelled as all the ladies stopped laughing and turned to chase him.

He and I ran from the kitchen and to the back den laughing our asses off as I thought how I was a lucky muthafucka.

Two hours later Ghost and I were high as hell and feeling like we had been on x all day as we found the ladies in the living room curled up on the couch. Tinka was asleep with her feet in Lilly's lap and just seeing that shit made me feel good.

"She passed out on our ass about 20 minutes in." Lilly whispered as I leaned over and picked Tinka up.

"Aite, goodnight y'all." Ghost said before we exchanged head nods and him and Belle disappeared to their side of the house.

I carried Tinka to bed as Lilly followed then laid her down gently on her side.

"So how do we do this? Should I sleep in here with y'all or go back to the couch?" Lilly whispered as she glanced over at our king-sized bed then back at me.

I was just about to answer when Tinka suddenly raised her head and spoke.

"Girl if you don't get your little thick ass in this bed and lay down. Quatty get yo ass in the middle so we'll both have access to you." Tinka said as she pulled back the covers on my side of the bed and I stripped down to my boxers before I got in and Lilly followed.

In seconds I was the meat in a fine female sandwich as Tinka curled up on me to the left and Lilly snuggled up on the right. They both laid their heads on my chest as I wrapped my arms around them then gently kissed their heads.

"A man can get used to this much love." I said as we all laughed then they both kissed me in sensitive spots on my chest.

I felt my dick jump at that moment and I closed my eyes trying to fight back the feelings. Even though I wanted nothing more than to fuck the life out of both of them, I didn't want to do it while Tinka was still pregnant. It just didn't seem right. That's why I laid there with my eyes closed while I held my breath and tried to suppress the urges running through me. I guess Tinka could feel the tension running through my arms as I flexed my muscles so she looked up at me and winked.

"We're all yours king so do what you feel. I see daddy woke down there. Let him out to play." Tinka said as she giggled and Lilly joined in.

I rubbed her back and laughed with them for a second before I told her I was happy so I was cool.

"I know fucking a pregnant girl with another girl may be a little weird, but you can go ahead and get your first night with Lilly. I'll still be here to make sure you both know I love you too." Tinka said as I looked down at her and kissed her passionately on the lips.

Lilly kissed my chest as I kissed Tinka and told them both I'd be happy just to sleep in their presence. That was enough to make them both melt in my arms and cover me with kisses until I damn near fell asleep. I was in such a lusty-love filled haze, I think I did doze off because the next thing I knew I was being awakened by a pair of soft, juicy lips on the head of my dick and another set on my neck.

"I want you to have her Quatty. You have been gone for too long. I want you to enjoy yourself and see why it's so important to stay out. We have a family now baby. We need you. We love you." Tinka said as she kissed my neck and I looked down at Lilly as she took my dick out of her mouth.

"We want you daddy." Lilly said in a seductive tone before she took my wood back into her mouth down to the balls and I fell back on the pillow and moaned.

After that they doubled teamed me with Tinka kissing my lips, whispering sweet nothings, and licking every sensitive spot on my neck and chest while Lilly gave me fire head. After about twenty minutes of that my dick was so hard that it throbbed and hurt. I damn near broke Lilly's back as Tinka called her up on top of me and she began to crawl up slowly with her eyes on mine.

I couldn't wait for that slow shit so I grabbed her hand and pulled her close enough that I could sit up a little and drag her up by her hips. In seconds, she was straddling me and I had her breasts in my mouth as her and Tinka kissed.

Maine, no lie, I cried like a baby when I saw that shit. There were my two bad bitches kissing as I sucked on titties like a starving calf. It was every niggas fantasy and my reality for the rest of my life. Considering the fucked up circumstances I had come from with a psycho bitch not letting go and trying to ruin my life, I figured I was doing good as fuck and I was enjoying every moment of it.

"Damn I'm a lucky muthafucka. Maine, I love you Tinka." I said as I suddenly came up from air and reached up to pull Tinka down to me to kiss.

I stuck my tongue down her throat and rubbed her titties as she moaned and Lilly rubbed my dick up her clit.

"I love you too baby, now fuck her. I checked, she clean. Welcome her into the family the right way daddy. Give her that dick." Tinka said taking me off guard as Lilly suddenly shoved all 11 inches of my dick inside of her wet, gooey center.

"Ahhh shit. I love you too Lilly." I said as I got so deep inside her wetness I felt no bottom and Tinka joined in our kiss.

I won't lie, I blacked out because all I remember is busting about six nuts back-to-back and waking up the next morning with a sore dick and a smile on my face. My ladies were up before me and I could hear them talking and singing in the kitchen as I got my clothes to shower.

After about twenty minutes in that bitch I came out feeling refreshed and ready to eat some shit up. I met Tinka as I walked down the hall towards the kitchen and she came towards me holding some homemade muffins.

"I was just coming to wake you up baby, before your food gets cold. Me and wifey been hooking it up. Now come on king and eat." Tinka said before she got on her tiptoes and gave me a juicy kiss.

I felt like a king for real as I walked in with her following me and telling me how much she loved me.

"I love you too Big Daddy Quatty. Now sit yo sexy ass down and eat." Lilly said as she came over and kissed me before sitting a fat ass plate in front of me.

I looked down at the bacon, sausage, pancakes, grits, fruit, eggs, and toast then back up at my ladies as they stood there side-by-side and smiled.

"Damn, all this for a G. I know I gotta stay my ass at home now." I said as I laughed and the ladies joined in as they sat down with their plates.

I sat there and laughed and talked with Lilly and Tinka as they each sat on one side of me and paused every few minutes to feed me.

"Damn, that's how it goes down now? Shit, I told you Belle you need a damn sister wife. Hell, I could be glowing and shit from a pussy feast this morning with two baddies feeding me. See? Yo ole stingy ass just won't let me be great." Ghost said as he and Belle walked into the kitchen and he saw what was going on.

I laughed at that nigga as Belle punched him in the back and then he came over to give me dap.

"Maine G, I promise I want to be just like you when I grow up." Ghost said as he sat down at the table across from me and Belle gave him his plate.

We joked and laughed as we all sat at the table and discussed our plans to move. Surprisingly, Lilly was more than willing to relocate so we set the date and time to go. Once we had that settled the ladies got up to wash dishes and me and Ghost disappeared to the garage to smoke and talk. As soon as we were inside and had fired up the first blunt, the real business was brought up and Beast Quatty was on high alert again.

"So, what we gonna do about Pooh? Do we leave and forget about the bitch? Or do we do what we do best and wipe her whole bloodline out then disappear? It's yo call homie, but you know I'm riding." Ghost said as he inhaled the loud smoke, held it, then handed the blunt to me.

I thought about all the shit I had done and seen since the drama started with Pooh as I hit the blunt and let it ease my mind. I had already risked and lost so much, I didn't want to go down that road again. I already knew Pooh wasn't worth my love or freedom, so I didn't want to give that hoe any more of my time and energy either. I was just tired and ready to move on to another phase in my life, one that didn't involve Pooh. That's why I told my nigga to focus on what was really important and let time work everything else out itself. That probably was my worse mistake.

"Nah fool, fuck that bitch. Let's just focus on getting our families out of Memphis and never look back. A hoe like Pooh will only end up one or two ways anyway, and that's dead or a junky. Let that hoe meet her fate on her own cause she ain't worth no more energy." I said to Ghost as he nodded but kept a skeptical expression on his face.

I could tell he didn't agree with that and he didn't believe it would work itself out. Truth be told, I felt that shit too but that optimistic Quatty within me just wouldn't die. That part of me that wanted so badly just to live happily and peacefully again, wouldn't let me see past the sunshine. All I could see was a happy life with Tinka, Lilly, and the kids, and that's all that I wanted to see.

"Besides nigga, I got too much fire pussy around me to worry about a washed out rotten hoe." I said as Ghost yelled out hell yeah and we both laughed.

Just then the door to the garage flew open and Tinka, Belle, and Lilly came in with their hands behind their backs. The expressions on their faces told me something was up so when they walked in I got up and prepared to run.

"What you get up for Quatty? We just came out to see what y'all were doing. We bored without y'all and since we don't smoke, we figured we'd come fuck with y'all." Tinka said smiling as she walked closer and I continued to back up.

"SOOOO, put y'all muthafucking hands up!" Lilly suddenly yelled when Tinka got within a foot of me and they all pulled out these huge as water guns.

Before I knew it me and Ghost were getting drenched and chasing the ladies around the house. Maine, it was like we were kids again running around and playing without a care in the world. The rest of our week was like that too; nothing but fun and happiness. During that week, we handled business, got the house packed up, and got the kid's withdrawal papers from school.

By Thursday I talked to Moe and he told me shit was back on track in jail. Wallace big punk ass was in protection but had already gotten shanked, fucked, and beat in the showers. He said the bitch begged for protection but he just laughed in his face. I laughed too hell. Knowing all the dirty Wallace had done, I was happy he was finally getting that shit right back.

Moe told me that wasn't the best part because business was better than ever too. He said he and Durty were back on top, had a new 'Lilly', and were recruiting new connects for when Durty got out. Moe reminded me about the P.O. Box and asked me if I had received the keys to the house his lawyer sent. I told him he had and thanked him for all he had done.

"No thanks needed nigga, we family. Just stay yo ass out of here. And when you find the instructions in the P.O. Box, hit me up and let's talk." Moe said and I told him I would before we hung up.

After that call, I was ready to go and start my new life. Saturday morning rolled around fast and I was ready to get it over with. When I got up, got dressed, and went into the living room, I found that everybody was already up and ready. Tinka had called Mazi Kyng Auto Transport to take the cars to the new house and had a huge van waiting on us outside.

"We're all ready to go King. The beds are staying so we don't have to worry about that and everything else is already on the way to the house. You ready to go?" Tinka asked me as she wrapped her arms around my neck and kissed me before I told her I was.

I had already said my goodbyes to my mother and sister, and had a smoke out with Peedy and the other homies. There was nothing else left for me in Memphis so I was happy as hell to turn around and take one last look at the house.

"Hell yeah I'm ready to go baby. I'm ready to leave all this shit behind." I said to Tinka as she stood in the doorway with me and Lilly walked up behind us.

Just as she got to us I could hear her phone ring from behind and then the stress in her voice after she answered the call.

"What bitch? Who is this? This gotta be that hoe Lay Lay because that cripple Pooh bitch can't dial a phone. What you want hoe and how you get my number?" Lilly yelled into the phone as me and Tinka turned around to look at her.

Tinka's little swollen belly ass got hyped instantly as she started yelling and cursing with Lilly into the phone.

"Y'all hoes ain't gonna do shit, ole punk ass bitches. Bitch I win and tell that shit bag having hoe that!" Tinka yelled as I grabbed her around the waist and told her to calm down.

I didn't want her getting so upset she went into labor and we would be forced to stay in Memphis longer. Hell no, that was the last thing I wanted so I quickly grabbed the phone from Lilly.

"Look bitch quit calling this phone because after this call it's over. You hoes should get a life or take care of yo damn kids. Tell Pooh, it's over and to just give up. Neither one of you hoes are worth our energy anymore so get the fuck on." I said ready to hang up when Lay Lay yelled my name.

"QUADERIOUS! Just remember I told you that you will regret this. We will destroy everything you love. Then we will see if it's worth it. BITCH!" Lay Lay said before she hung up the phone and I couldn't do shit but laugh.

I laughed at how psycho them bitches were and how they had nothing better to do with their time. I should have been taking heed to what the hoe said though, but I was too focused to care.

"From this point on, we leave all this bullshit behind." I said as I closed the door, locked it, put the key in the mailbox like the real estate agent had said, and then chunked Lilly's phone into the street.

I wanted the calls to end and any memory of Pooh so I had to get rid of Lilly's phone just like I had done Tinka's. I told her I would buy her another one when we got to Charlotte as she smiled and told me she didn't care before she kissed me on the neck.

"Today ladies, we start our new lives. Let's go and be happy. I love y'all." I said as Tinka and Lilly both grabbed one of my hands and we walked off the porch together, determined to live better than we ever had before.

# Chapter 10

The ride from Memphis to Charlotte was long but fun as fuck. I drove as Ghost sat on the passenger side and Belle's sons, Ty and Sean, sat behind us and rapped. Them young niggas had us rolling for hundreds of miles as they rap checked each other and everyone we passed by. We stopped to eat a few times and had several bathroom breaks but we still made it to Charlotte in less than 9 hours because me and Ghost took turns pushing the van to 90 on the highway. We pulled into downtown Charlotte at a little after 8 that evening and I drove right to the address Moe had given me.

When we pulled up on the block and saw all of the million dollar homes and well-manicured lawns we knew we were a long way from Memphis. It was like a whole different world and even though I had lived in both the hood and some nice neighborhoods in Memphis, I had never seen wealthy like the wealthy Charlotte had to offer. That was some shit I could get used to. I pulled into the driveway and cut the van off before I looked over at Ghost.

"What the fuck bruh?" Ghost said as he looked at me then the huge, two story mansion with what seemed to be two separate houses attached.

I won't lie, I was shocked as hell too as I sat there holding the steering wheel looking from Ghost to the house.

"I know right bruh. This shit huge. I had no idea Moe was living like this. Well, he would have been living like this had he not gotten flapped. Maine, this like a dream and the nigga gave it to us? We gotta check this shit out. Let's let the women and children sleep as we secure the mutha fucking premises." I said jokingly as me, Ghost, Ty, and Sean got out of the van quietly and walked up the circle driveway to the house.

Even the front of that muthafucka was fyre with Koi ponds, big ass sculptures like on Scarface, and these damn marble, crystal stones on the walkway. I felt like Prince Akeem walking down that bitch and towards the house that was mine.

"Maine this shit look like Reverend Run house. Like that shit on MTV Cribs." Ty said as Sean agreed and I laughed.

I agreed with them young niggas as I walked pass them dipping their hands in the Koi pond out front and made my way to the emergency box next to the door Moe said the key was in. I ran my hand along the back of it, knocked two times on the side, then pressed, pulled and released the latch on the box just like Moe said and there the key and code to the alarm was.

"Like butter baby." I said to Ghost in my Peedy's voice as he laughed and I laughed my way over to open the door.

Maine, when I opened that door and we walked in, I think we all reverted back to preschool kids. It was so beautiful with the vaulted ceilings, crown molding and huge flat screens and projectors already mounted on the walls, we couldn't help but to run through that bitch. After I cut off the alarm, I checked out the huge dining room, family room, din, theatre, gourmet kitchen, and three bathrooms on the first floor before I jetted off to the next level.

Upstairs the master suite took up most of the entire floor with two huge walk in closets, dual master baths, and a reader nook in the corner. Moe had the house fully furnished on the upper levels too with a huge California King bed still in plastic in the master suite. I flopped in that bitch and almost fell asleep it was so soft. I think I may have dozed off for real though because the next thing I knew Ghost's old excited ass was there kicking the bottom of my shoe and screaming my name.

"QUATTY! Fool get yo ass up. This shit like four buildings in the projects big fool. Come on. Look at this shit." Ghost said as I got up and followed him out of the room.

There was three more big bedrooms and two baths on that level with the master suite, along with a laundry room.

"Damn, that's how rich people do it? I already saw a laundry room downstairs, and its two kitchens. Check this shit out." Ghost said as he ran his happy ass down the steps and I followed.

He was right too because when we got back down the steps we turned right and walked down a short hall into one of those wings I thought were separate houses from the outside. The one on the right was like a huge three-bedroom house in Memphis with two bathrooms, a living room and separate kitchen. That bitch was fully furnished too with huge beds and flats on the wall.

"Goddam fool. This bitch bigger than my mama house." I said as me and Ghost laughed and I followed him down the long hall just off the bathroom.

That hall led all the way across to the other wing of the house where there was two more bedrooms, a bathroom and sunroom.

"NIGGA WE MADE IT!" Ghost yelled out when we walked out of that wing and into the huge back yard with pool, jacuzzi, playground and basketball court.

"Hell yeah we did fool. I think this shit bigger than T.I. house." I said as me and Ghost laughed like little ass girls until Ty and Sean finally found us.

We all checked out the backyard and damn near took a dip in the pool before I remembered the sleeping women we left in the van.

"Damn fool, we out here enjoying and shit. We forgot all about Tinka, Belle, Lilly, Sasha, and Damieon out in the van. We tripping." I said as I turned and made my way through the huge house and out into the front yard.

I got back in the van, drove it up the driveway, and started to unloaded the bags before any other them even heard me. Ghost and I were carrying in the last things when Tinka finally woke up and called my name.

"Quatty, where we at? The hotel? I thought we were going to the house." Tinka said as she opened the door and stepped out slowly, stretching her cramped muscles with her hand on her stomach.

Ghost and I stood there smiling as we watched her stretch and reach into the van to touch the other ladies and wake them before she turned to get a good look at where we were. When she did, the happiness she felt was apparent in her eyes as they danced and tears began to fall.

"QUATTTYYYY. Are you serious? This can't be our house. Quatty, really?" Tinka said as she ran over to me and wrapped her arms around my neck.

I wiped away her tears and kissed her face as I shook my head yes.

"Yes baby, I'm serious. This is our new house. Our lives are about to be much different now baby. Better. I promise." I told Tinka before I kissed her lips and held her tight.

Seconds later Belle, Lilly, Damieon, and Sasha were out of the van and on their feet gawking at the massive house in front of them.

"Really daddy?" Lilly said as she came over with Damieon in her arms and they both looked at me smiling in anticipation.

Damieon couldn't contain his happiness as he giggled and shook in Lilly's arms, waiting on me to confirm.

"Really daddy Quatty?" He asked as I reached over and rubbed his little curly head.

Damieon and I had become just as close as Lilly and I had so his little smile melted my damn heart. I reached over and grabbed him out of Lilly's arms as I told her yes and she kissed my lips before her, Tinka, Lilly, and Sasha ran into the house.

"Maine, ain't shit like seeing your family smile G. Now, I see what you were talking about. We gotta keep this shit going bruh and don't fuck up our good things." Ghost said to me before he gave me dap then me and a giggling Damieon followed him into the house as I tickled him.

"You know you right about that bruh. Our women are worth all the shit we been through and anything we can give them. We gotta make this shit last forever. They deserve happiness. Hell, we do too." I said to Ghost as I closed the door and stepped into my new life.

Happiness was all I had from that day forward too, just sunshine and smiles. The next day Ghost and I made our way to the post office while the ladies unpacked all of the stuff the movers had brought, getting the house ready for our baby's arrival.

At the post office, I went inside and got the P.O. Box contents which was a black duffle bag filled with $1 million dollars in cash, and several manila envelopes. After I opened that damn bag and saw its contents, I didn't even care about what was in the envelopes I just wanted to get the fuck out of there before somebody figured out it was a mistake or some shit. That's what I did too and when I ran back out to the car like a fucking scolded cat, Ghost could tell something was up.

"Damn wasup bruh? You rob that bitch or something?" He asked as I jumped in and threw the bag and envelopes in his lap.

I waited until he opened the bag and peeked inside before I crunk up the van and prepared to pull off.

"BRUUUHHHHH. I know this ain't what the fuck I think it is." Ghost said as I shook my head yes and said it was one million dollars in cash.

Maine, you would have thought we had robbed that bitch for real after I said that because Ghost instantly zipped the bag back up and started looking around as he told me to pull the fuck off. I didn't waste any time doing that either as I swung that big muthafucka out of the spot and sped towards the house. I felt numb but light as a feather while we drove and Ghost talked as he went through the envelopes.

"Yeah, we set for life now bruh. We gotta get Peedy nem down here now. And make sure we spread some love to our brothers back home and locked up. The jail gonna---" Ghost said and suddenly stopped as he pulled a piece of paper out of one of the envelopes.

I drove and looked over at him every two seconds as he read a piece of paper that made him laugh.

"Maine fool, yo cousin a muthafucking genius. Do you know what this is I'm holding in my hand nigga?" Ghost said as I shook my head no and he continued.

"Well, you know how you told me what went down with Wallace right?" Ghost said as I shook my head yes and he kept going.

"Well nigga, while you and Lilly was getting info and setting him up on that rape shit, Moe was digging for the paper trial. That nigga found that Wallace bitch offshore account with $4.2 million dollars of stolen money in it that is supposedly untraceable. This fucking letter here says," Ghost said as he picked up another letter he had taken out the envelope.

"This one says we should wait at least one year before trying to get the money because it still may be a little hot. The account is in a lady's name, Lillian Burrows, so we will need a female to do the transaction when we do get ready to do it. It's just our luck one of your wives name is Lilly. Dammnnn bruh. I can't even believe this shit." Ghost said as he sat back in the passenger seat with the letters still in hand, stunned.

I was stunned as fuck too knowing that million we were holding wasn't even a piece of the money we were sure to see. I had to sit there and concentrate on driving as I got my thoughts together and Ghost went through the other envelop that was filled with diamonds and jewels and another one containing papers.

"Aye bruh, damn. This ain't even the half of it G." Ghost said as he sat back up and told me what the letter said.

"This a letter straight from Moe that say its 30 keys buried in the backyard. He said it's enough dope there for you to take over any major city and become the man. Maine bruh, we on for real now." Ghost said excited while some of my joy melted.

I didn't want to fuck with the dope game anymore and risk losing all we had. I told that nigga that too and he sat there and thought about it until we pulled up at the house.

"You right bruh. I was the one just talking about us doing right. How about you tell Moe we ain't ready for that and we sit on this shit until we ready to get the money from that account. Then we'll decide. That's straight cause I see yo big head ass over there stressing nigga." Ghost said laughing as he got out the van and I breathed a sigh of relief.

I was already nervous as hell knowing we had all that money and millions more to get. I didn't want the drama that dope game could bring so I was glad Ghost had dropped that shit. I got out the van in front of the house feeling like I really belonged there. I walked into the house with a smile on my face and excitement in my step I couldn't hide. When I told the family what had happened that happiness spread like the plague and we stayed that way until the following week, July 20th to be exact, when my daughter was born.

The day my daughter, Amira Jaye, was born had to be the scariest yet happiest day of my life. It was a Friday and everyone was home from work and school. Tinka and I had opened a full-service salon and boutique, and me and Ghost had just taken over several laundromats and corner stores in one of Charlotte's hoods. Shit was good so that was a day of rest to finally settle into our new house and life. Tinka and I had just come down stairs that morning and sat at the table to eat when she got a pain so vicious that knocked her off her chair.

"Tinka baby, what's wrong?" I yelled as I jumped up and everyone else ran around us.

My heart raced and I felt light headed as fuck when I bent down to rub her head.

"Baby, I think it's time Quatty. Go get my bag." Tinka yelled at me and Ghost helped her to her feet and as soon as she was in an upright position, water rushed down her leg like a water fountain.

"Oh shit! What the fuck?" I yelled shocked as hell and Ghost yelled out too.

Lilly and Belle laughed at our dumb asses as they pushed us away and grabbed Tinka by both arms to walk her out to my truck which had been delivered.

"Y'all muthafuckas so stupid, ole shaky asses. Her water just broke. Quatty. QUATTY! Snap out of it ole shocked ass nigga and go get her bag. Ghost you get on out and crank the truck up. Ty, you're in charge. Sean, Sasha, and Damieon listen to Ty. Now come on y'all." Belle said as she barked out orders while Tinka panted and Lilly helped her with her breathing.

Belle's aggressiveness was what I needed though to snap my ass out of it because after that I was up the steps in a flash and coming down with the bag. I got out to the truck in six seconds and got us to the hospital in what seemed to be four. All the while I drove Tinka panted in the back seat as Belle rubbed her head and Lilly held her hand and helped her to breathe.

I kept my eyes rotating from the rear-view mirror to look at Tinka, to the road in front of me, and Ghost ole hyperventilating ass in the passenger seat. I knew I was fucked up and scared as held but on the outside I was holding my shit together. Ghost on the other hand though, that chocolate bastard was four shades of white as he pressed his face up against the window and groaned.

"Ugghhh bruh, I can't take this shit. What's happening now? Why she breathing like that? Is the baby coming out? Quatty punch this bitch!" Ghost yelled frantically as he quickly looked in the backseat before he turned back to the window.

I couldn't do shit but laugh as I sped up a little ready to get to the hospital and meet my little girl. Seeing my nigga, the killer, so fucked up behind that gave me strength and I was able to shake off my anxiety and focus on my joy.

By the time I pulled up at the hospital I was cool, calm, and collected as I got out, told Ghost to go get a wheelchair, then walked around to help Lilly and Belle get Tinka out. She was stretched out on the seat with her legs wide open by the time I came around and I swear to God I saw my daughter's head peeking out of that pink starburst. That put my ass into overdrive so I reached in and whisked Tinka up in my arms to carry her inside.

"I love you baby." I whispered to her as I carried her in and Belle yelled she was going to park the truck.

"I love you too baby and I can't wait to meet this perfect combination of us. Now hurry QUATTTYYY." Tinka yelled as we ran inside and I saw Ghost running full speed towards us with a wheelchair.

He got within six feet of us with the chair when he fell face first and the chair went rolling down the hall. At that moment, none of us could hold our laughter, not even the doctors coming to get Tinka or Tinka herself. We all cracked the fuck up as they put Tinka on a stretcher and told us she was already in labor. She was rushed directly to the back and I was taken to the adjoining room to clean up and put on scrubs. By the time, I made it in the delivery room they had Tinka hooked up to about eight machines, legs wide open and she was pushing.

"Come on daddy." Lilly said as she stood beside Tinka and held her hand.

I smiled to myself knowing she had asked for Lilly to come back so that all of the parents were there. I joined Lilly beside Tinka as I stood behind her head and rubbed her hair and I told her I loved her. In minutes the doctor was there and introduced herself before she told Tinka to push.

Now, I had seen several births on T.V. before, hell I had even been in the room with my sister when she had her babies. However, Tinka's actual birth was different from all of those because it was over in a second. Before I knew it that thang was opening up like a stretched out as turtle neck and a beautiful, big, pink, baby with thick curly hair was coming out. I don't even know what came over me when I saw that but suddenly all of that squeamish shit was gone. I wanted nothing more than to be up in the mix so I went around to the end of the table by the doctor to get involved. I wanted my daughter to see me first because I was the only male face she would see the rest of her life. I refused to be anything like my father because I was going to have both of my families; wives and kids included, under one roof with me. I reached out and grabbed the scissors after the doctor handed them to me to cut the umbilical cord. When I cut that cord, I think I cut all ties to my old life and became a new, better Quatty instantly. That beautiful little girl I had helped bring into the world was my priority and she was worth it.

"She is gorgeous. I love you Amira Jaye." I said as I looked at Tinka and I could tell that she loved the name.

We had decided not to name the baby until we saw it and that was the name that felt right to me. I named her Amira because it was Tinka's mama's name and Jaye because that was Peanut, my best friend who I killed, first name. I felt like we both still had ties to those we loved by giving our daughter that name. I could tell Tinka thought that too as she cried and shook her head as she smiled.

"Amira. Mommy loves you." Tinka whispered after I brought the baby over and she kissed her head.

Lilly got her kisses in too after I handed the baby to Tinka and stood back to watch the three women I loved the most. It was a beautiful sight, one that I wanted to see for the rest of my life. After that they cleaned Amira up then the rest of the family came in to see its newest member. Damioen loved his little sister right from the start too and their bond was undeniable as Amira opened her eyes and smiled when he held her.

Life was truly bliss for a year after that with me and Ghost getting engrossed in and growing our businesses and the ladies making Tinka's spot in Charlotte the biggest and baddest salon, boutique in the state. I felt I was complete at that point, the only thing that was missing was making it official. We did that in September of that next year, right after Amira's first birthday. Tinka and I wanted to include Lilly so we had a triple wedding in Fernando de Noronha, Brazil on Baía do Sancho beach.

It was beautiful out on the water with all of our family and friends around us. We flew in everybody; my mama and sister, Peedy and Twala, Lilly's parents, and a few more cousins and homies from the block. I stood out on the beach in my white linen suit with Gucci shoes and accents as my best men; Peedy and Ghost stood on each side of me.

My heart melted when my daughter walked down
the aisle throwing flowers and her brother Damieon, now 6
followed carrying the ring. Everyone's smiles and the
wonderful scenery had my ass misty eyed by the time the
music started and Ty walked Tinka down the aisle with
Lilly and her father behind. No lie, I cried like a baby when
I saw their beautiful asses in those white dresses, hair and
face on fleek, with smiles and tears in their eyes. I had to
hold on to Ghost as they got closer and everything seemed
to swirl fast around my head.

"It's just yo nerves nigga. You good. You wonna back out
with all that pussy coming towards you?" Ghost whispered
as Peedy agreed and we all laughed.

Like always, my homies were by my side and them
niggas gave me the strength I needed to stand the fuck up
and grab the hands of my wives. I stared at them both
looking all gorgeous before I lifted their veils and stood
between them. The minister said a few words then married
me and Tinka followed by a commitment ceremony
between all three of us.

We walked off that beach that day; three people as
one with nothing but hope for the future. Our future was
great after that too because everybody in the family was
grinding. Ty had graduated with a full basketball
scholarship to the University of North Carolina and Sean
and Sasha were doing good. All of our businesses were
flourishing and my relationship with my wives were better
than ever. There was no darkness in our lives except for
when I went out into the backyard and remembered what
was buried beneath it. I don't know why, but I just felt like
some day, some kind of way that shit would fuck me over.
Moe had been bugging me to dig it up and do something
with it since I had gotten to Charlotte. I told him I didn't
want to do it and even tried to give it to Durty when him
and Yada came down, but Moe said he had given it to me.

"I just want to make sure you straight cousin. Durty already heavy out there. You can give him something but keep the majority for you. Just in case. Believe me cuzzo, dirty money lasts much longer than clean. Hell, our country was built on it. Just sit on it then my nigga. You will figure something out." Moe said the last time we talked and that was a year before my wedding.

Two years after that I still hadn't touched that shit and I really didn't plan too. I had a three-year-old daughter, eight-year-old son, two wives, eight businesses, and was worth over $8 million dollars, four of which I still hadn't touched yet. Hell, I was winning so I had no intentions of grabbing that dope and doing anything with it unless I was giving it to Durty.

Durty and Yada had been down to kick it and grind at least four times a year since our wedding, and I couldn't think of a better person to give it to. That would be the perfect way to ensure my nigga stayed straight and was the only way that I could keep away from all bullshit. That was my only focus. I had made it almost four years with no drama, no darkness and most of all no Pooh. In my eyes, I was living on a cloud and nothing could bring me down.

I found out just how wrong I was about that on August 15th when I was sitting in the office at the house working on some advertising for our laundry mats and I got a poke on Facebook. I stopped what I was doing to see who had poked me and when I clicked the notification my heart stopped. The name on the profile said nothing but *MiMi Baby*, yet I still knew it was Pooh. I didn't even have to click the profile to know that it was her but when I did I was glad that I did. I scrolled that hoe's timeline quickly and all I could see was subliminal and upfront posts about me. It had been four years, four long years, yet that bitch still hadn't given up.

"What the fuck?" I said to myself out loud as I sat up in my chair and took off my glasses.

I bit my bottom lip and tried to suppress that beast Quatty who was pushing his way to the surface, as I scrolled back up to her page to read her most recent posts.

Her most recent post read, *I see you, but you don't see me*, and I don't know why but that shit made the hair on my arms stand up. I had to close my eyes and concentrate on my breathing as my rage kept trying to break free. When I opened my eyes back up I scrolled down to the post right before that one and I couldn't help but to feel nervous when I saw a pic of what appeared to be the coffee shop close to my house.

I clicked the picture and blew that bitch up trying to find anything distinctive that would tell me it was that coffee shop for sure. I guess that bitch planned on me doing that though because she had cropped the pic in a way that the sign or anything around it wasn't visible. I didn't have to see it though because that feeling in my gut told me it was along with that stupid ass caption she put on the picture.

*Sitting out scoping in the rain on my Blues Clues Shit. Trying to make all the pieces to the puzzle fit and make him see she ain't worth it,* the post read and that was enough to make me dismiss paranoia and try to get some answers. I deactivated my Facebook page after that before I made a fake one then called Peedy. I had to know what was going on at that moment back home and he was the right man to get it. I know I sounded Irate and irritated as fuck when he answered the phone and I just started going the fuck off.

"Maine, I tried so hard to change and leave all that bullshit behind me. I been doing good to G, on my shit getting back everything I lost. Now this shit pops up and I know I'm about to have to go back into beast mode. I can just feel it my nigga." I said rambling as my thoughts jumbled together and my anger overpowered all logic.

I loved my family too much to let Pooh come along again and destroy it all. I had spared her life many times in the past, but I knew that if she did anything to harm my family I couldn't do that again. I didn't want to go there though and that's why I needed answers.

"Maine, wasup Quatty? What you talkin about nigga?" Peedy asked confused as I told him what happened.

Suddenly he had urgency in his voice after he heard that and he told me he would put his ear to the street.

"Maine, I ain't heard shit about that bitch in a while, not since she got out the wheelchair and shit. She was back to old Pooh at that point and I thought she had forgot about you. I guess the hoe just couldn't find you. Facebook a muthafucka though bruh. Anyway, I'll find out and if she here in the M, she good as gone. That's my word. "Peedy said before he hung up and I sat back in my chair.

I told Ghost about what happened later that night and for three days we were on high alert. We didn't tell the ladies because we didn't want to scare them, but we got ready for whatever. I broke down and dug up Moe's stash to retrieve the dope and guns. I gave the dope to Ghost to hide somewhere else and got everyone capable in the house strapped just in case without them even knowing trouble was lurking. Pooh was so unpredictable I wasn't taking any chances and I would body that bitch if I had to.

Four days after that poke and nothing else from Pooh and no word from Peedy we all began to relax again. I was back going to the gym mid-day before I picked up Amira and Damieon from school. That day in particular, I left a bit late and when I got about a block away from the gym, I noticed this little blue car trailing three cars behind me. I spotted that muthafucka out of all the cars on the street because I had seen it about four times before.

Whenever I left the gym or Amira and Damieon's school I would see that car riding by or behind me at the light. The tint was so dark I could never see inside but I knew it was the same car. That never bothered me before because I knew a lot people from my neighborhood had kids in their school, but after the incident with Pooh that shit seemed fishy. That's why as I approached the yellow light at a major interception I punched that bitch and ran through the light just before it changed.

I looked in my rearview as I drove down the street and saw the little blue car trying to maneuver through traffic to get closer to the light. It was too late though because I was already turning the corner. I laughed to myself as I drove closer to the school, thinking how stupid I must have looked running from a car that probably wasn't even chasing me with my paranoid ass. I was so caught up in my laughter that I almost ran into the back of a pickup truck as I approached the stalled traffic. A wreck had everyone backed up for blocks so I put my shit in park and then turned around trying to see if I could make a U-turn. I quickly saw there was no hope though with blocks of traffic behind me. It was no way around it at that point, I was stuck.

"Damn, come on y'all. It's almost 3." I said out loud to myself as I punched the steering wheel and looked around.

There was nowhere for me to go but up on the sidewalk and I didn't want to do that and risk getting arrested. I sat there, stuck for damn near twenty minutes still kinda bothered by that damn blue car with a nagging feeling in my heart, before I went up over the curb and got the fuck out. The police and other emergency personnel were so busy with the wreck at that point that they didn't even notice me bucking the system. I was glad too as I sped down the street headed right to the school.

I got there at 3:34 and I damn near hopped the curb again as I pulled in front of the school. I jumped out even more upset after I saw that Amira and Damieon weren't outside waiting with their teacher. When I was later before she said that was what she would do if it happened again so I couldn't understand where they were. I ran into the building in old Quatty speed and made it to the office just as the teacher and Damieon were walking out.

"Oh, hi Mr. Jones. I was just about to call you. I was wondering who was picking Damieon up since one of your wives already got Amira." The teacher said and my fucking heart stopped because I knew I was supposed to get them.

"What do you mean? Which one of my wives?" I asked as the teacher helped Damieon put on his backpack.

"Oh, it was Nicole sir in the gray Benz. I remember seeing her big pretty red fro." The teacher said smiling as I looked at her crazy knowing Tinka had changed her hairstyle the night before.

I grabbed Dameion's hand without saying another word to the teacher as we ran out of the school and to the car. I pulled out my phone as soon as I put him in and instantly dialed Tinka's number while I closed the door.

"Please tell me you got Amira." Was all I said when Tinka answered the phone and when she said no my whole world came crashing down around me once again.

# Chapter 11

"What baby? Please don't be playing right now. Tell me if you have Amira." I said to Tinka as I hopped in the car and told Damieon to buckle up before I crunk up and sped off.

My heart was pounding and mind was racing as I rode towards home, searching the streets for signs of the blue car.

"No Quatty baby, I don't have her and neither does Belle, Sasha, or Lilly. Were' all here at the store working. We thought you were getting them. Where is my baby Quatty?" Tinka yelled as I heard hysteria creep into her voice.

That was the same hysteria I was feeling inside as I drove like a maniac through the streets. I knew what had happened at that point, Pooh had my baby and I was determined to get her back.

"All y'all get to the house now. That bitch back and I think she has Amira." I said to Tinka as I heard her break down.

I couldn't even listen to that shit or I would have crashed so I hung up and threw the phone into the passenger seat. Tears and violent body jerks hit me suddenly as I pulled into the yard and Damieon jumped out. I cried and punched the steering wheel and the dash as I asked God why.

"Why? What the fuck? Lord, please protect my baby. Lord please forgive me too because I'm bodying this bitch!" I yelled to myself as Ghost suddenly snatched open the car door asking me what had happened.

Damioen had ran in to get him from the house when he saw how distraught I was. I hated I had let him see me so upset but I just couldn't hold back what I was feeling. Knowing Pooh and what she was capable of, I was terrified for my angel. I was terrified for her too because the fire had been lit inside me when she touched my child. There was no putting it out until everything in her world was destroyed.

"What happened Quatty? Wasup bruh?" Ghost said as I jumped out of the car and rushed past him into the house.

I told him everything that went down and that Amira was gone as I went to the secret safe room behind the floor length mirror in the dining room and started getting out guns.

"That bitch touched my baby fool. Ain't no more understanding. Everybody dies and then we disappear. This shit ends now, but if anything happens to my baby that whole fucking city burns. THAT'S MY WORD." I yelled as I cried and snot ran all down my face like Trey on Boyz in the Hood.

My nigga came over to hug me as he cried too and told me we would get her back.

"It's nonstop now bruh. Never touch a man's family. That hoe has to die, no questions asked. And so, does anyone related to her. Get shit packed up and ready to go bruh. Let me make the calls. I'll call Peedy right now and make him find out. 12 bruh, we gonna get her back. This shit about to end." Ghost said with his forehead pressed up against mine as he palmed the top of my head and cried.

"We in this together bruh, till the end. I got you. We soldiers and we gonna find the princess. Let's go nigga." Ghost said as I sucked up my tears and wiped my face while the girls rushed in.

Tinka and Lilly ran straight to my arms hysterical as Sasha swept up Damieon in her arms and took him upstairs. I held my ladies as Belle and Ghost cursed on their phones and gave orders, and I thought about my sweet, little

Amira. I thought about her beautiful face, long curly hair, and melodic laugh. I thought about how sweet and trusting she was and how a person like Pooh loved to prey on the weak.

As I stood there and held Tinka and Lilly in my embrace, and the boys rushed into the house, I prayed that the Lord wouldn't make Amira pay for my sins. I knew that a lot of my actions meant bad karma was looking for me, I just hoped it hadn't found my daughter instead. I hadn't done anything that bad in my life to someone who didn't deserve it, to be dealing with some heavy shit like I was. That shit was so overwhelming I almost spazzed out until I looked down into the distraught faces of Tinka and Lilly. They were looking to me for guidance and to lead my family in the right way. They expected me to be the man, or better yet the beast, that they knew I could be when provoked. That's exactly who I was too. I was going to eradicate everything in my way to getting my baby back. Anything.

"Okay babies, this the deal. Come on now, we gotta be strong about this. We getting our baby back so I need both of you in beast mode. This shit right here has kicked off a plan that's really been in the making four years so I need y'all with me." I said as I stood back and held their faces up in my hand.

Both of them felt my love and strength at that moment and I saw it all in their eyes.

"Now, we about to go to Memphis, we leaving all kids here. This is a blackout mission so if you don't think you have the heart to kill now, this is the time to say so." I said to them both and they gave me the answer with their eyes.

Their eyes told me that just like me, they would kill anyone to get Amira back. Belle left nothing to speculation though as she walked over and put her two cents in.

"I'll kill a nun in the fucking church if she fucks with my family. Let's ride nigga, I already got word on the hoe. I called my bitch who works for the airline and she pulled up the flight plans. She said a bitch bought a ticket for herself and a child about a month ago, that was set to leave at 4 this afternoon going to Memphis one way. That had to be Pooh and that means the bitch will be back in Memphis in about five hours with the layover. I got hittas on guard at the airport so hopefully we will get the bitch before she gets off the lot. We gotta move though." Belle said in beast mode like a muthafucka.

I liked that shit, she fed the beast in me so I turned around to give that fire to my ladies. I didn't have to though because they were on go after that as they told me let's ride. Belle told the boys what to do while we were gone as Ghost yelled out that Peedy and Durty had the soldiers on alert around the city. I told him to call our police homies to set up diversions as I got my guns and headed to the truck. Everybody followed me and once everyone was inside I crunk up and sped the fuck off. I filled the ladies in on the plan as we sped out of our quiet, rich little suburb headed right back into the belly of the beast, determined to save our princess.

"Okay so this the plan. We gonna get there and we going straight to Lay Lay's house if they ain't caught them at the airport. We kill everybody in that bitch except Lay Lay because she know where Pooh at. Once we find that out, that bitch gone and we move on to the next target. Once we have our baby back safe and sound with us we jet straight back here to get our shit and get ghost. The kids packing the vitals now and I texted L to put the house on the market. We bought a Villa in Bora Bora a year ago and that's where we're all relocating. Now, one important order of business when we get our baby back and get back here will be Lilly going to the bank with this ID I got her and getting the $4.2 million we have in an account. I'll explain all that shit to y'all afterwards, you just have to trust me for now. Now, I handled all our finances too and they're already in off shore accounts. So, clear your minds of everything and focus on nothing but getting our baby back. This bitch stepped over a line no one should ever cross and her whole family gotta pay for that." I said as I pushed the truck a little faster and bolted down the interstate.

We got to Memphis in six hours flat, I don't know how me and Ghost didn't get pulled over by the state troopers as fast as we were going. I guess the Gods opened up the highway for us because we slid through traffic without any issues as I kept my mind on my daughter. I had wondered what was happening to her as the four-hour mark of their flight approached and I was still at least an hour and a half away from the city.

That's why once I saw that sign saying welcome to Memphis I was in Gorilla mode with zero understanding. I couldn't forgive myself if anything happened to my baby because of that bitch. It would be like I was gone too because without her I was nothing. That's all I could think about as I drove towards Peedy's garage so we could jump in our steamers. Peedy and six other homies were waiting on us outside as we all jumped out dressed in black and ready to burn the fucking city down.

"Damn Quatty, Tinka. We finna find Amira. Now, they didn't catch them at the airport because TSA flapped the homies for suspicion because they were lurking around. We did just get word though that Lay Lay got a little house out in South Haven and she at the house. Chances are Pooh there because I heard the bitch had moved out of town. Possibly to North Carolina to be closer to you and pull this shit off. That's a rotten hoe my nigga but tonight this shit ends. We ready folk. I love you brother." Peedy said as he showed me love.

I shook up with the other brothers too as Ghost answered a call on his phone. A couple seconds later he told me we were all clear on the Memphis police for an hour but we were on our own in South Haven. I didn't give a fuck about that though because I planned on getting in and out without a trace. In my heart, I already knew Pooh wasn't there but I knew I could find out where she was through Lay Lay. I was gonna tortured that rotten bitch the same way her and Pooh had done me. I didn't want Tinka, Belle, and Lilly taking that ride so after Peedy gave me the keys to a low key, black Maximum I gave them to Tinka and told her to patrol the city.

"You remember all the hoe old spots right, ride by and see what's shaking. Keep y'all guns cocked and stay on go." I told Tinka before I kissed her then walked around to kiss Lilly.

"And shoot anybody in her bloodline. No survivors." Ghost yelled as I kissed Lilly then they pulled off.

We were on go after that as I got the address from Peedy and told them to follow us to the spot. Peedy gave us the keys to a black Tahoe and me and Ghost jumped in with guns and ammo on deck. I told Ghost to load the guns with silencers on them as I got on the expressway headed to South Haven. We made it to that bitch and in front of the little two-bedroom Lay Lay and all her damn kids lived in at about midnight. I pulled three houses past that bitch's house into an abandoned lot and turned the truck off as Peedy and the crew pulled up in front of us. Ghost and I jumped out with the bags and masks in hand and signaled for them to come around the house.

"Okay, y'all niggas cover the perimeter, anybody come out you use these." I said as I handed them all guns with silencers on them then we all put on our masks.

"No noise and no trace niggas. Act like we back on the block and the op is out to get us. Peedy, you come in with me and Ghost, we're going to find Lay Lay." I said as everybody nodded their heads and went to post up.

I breathed deeply and exhaled some of my hate as I stormed towards the front door. As we rounded the house I could hear Lay Lay, the voice of a nigga and another bitch along with the giggles of kids. I stopped for a second at the steps when I thought about killing them when I was trying to save my own child. That conscious, moral part of me wanted to say let the kids live, but my niggas weren't having that.

"Don't start that shit nigga. This ain't no time to have a conscious." Peedy whispered as he nudged me from the back.

I took one step up on to the porch after that but stopped as my mind continued to wonder. The conscious is a muthafucka sometimes because even though I knew I didn't give a fuck about them kids when it came to mine, my morals just kept being a bitch and popping up. Ghost had something for that though as he stepped up on to the step with me and whispered in my ear.

"They lives more important than Amira's?" He asked as I suddenly snapped my head around to look at him as tears began to build up in my eyes.

He could see in my eyes that was not the case even though he knew it already. He also knew him talking to me like that would amp me up and sure as shit stanks it did.

"That's all I'm saying nigga. No, them little shit eaters ain't more important than Amira. Remember they will grow up to be psycho muthafuckas just like they're mammies so we're going the world a favor. Suck that moral shit up Quatty. Beast Mode to find the princess." Ghost said and once again I was on go.

I mobbed up the rest of the steps without warning and crept open the screen door as I put my ear to it to listen. I could hear everyone still in there in the same positions so I turned to whisper orders.

"The bitch and the nigga over here on the couch, take the nigga out first." I whispered pointing to the left wall by the window where I could see the couch they were sitting on.

"The kids over here in the floor so they will be easy. Lay Lay in the kitchen. I want that hoe alive until she tells me what I need to know." I said to my niggas as they nodded and then I turned around with the shit.

I kicked that bitch in so fast and with so much force the door flew forward and knocked one of Lay Lay's little boy's on his ass. We didn't even give them time to react after that before we came in that bitch dumping. Ghost slumped that nigga off the muscle with a bullet to the forehead and I caught the bitch as she tried to run into the kitchen.

Lay Lay heard the shots and came to see what it was when I met her in the doorway. That bitch turned ghost white before my eyes as I smiled at her and showed her my gun. I think she shitted on herself after that as shots rang out and her kids screamed. I could see slight devastation in her glossy, drugged out eyes because she knew they were gone. Suddenly, one who got away came running through the kitchen and down the hall, and I turned to look as Lay Lay slipped away.

I didn't chase her ass though, I just laughed that evil Durty laugh that seemed to echo throughout the house as she ran and snatched the back door open. Right then I knew why my laugh was so boisterous as Durty lifted Lay Lay up by the neck and threw her ass back into the house. He continued to laugh like a psycho as he came inside and closed the door behind him. I watched as Lay Lay crawled backwards away from Durty, terrified at what he would do. She should have been too because that nigga was a maniac, what she didn't know was that I was even worse. I kicked that bitch in the back of the head with the Timberlands I had on and damn near broke her neck.

"Get up you maggot ass bitch. Where the fuck my baby at? Y'all hoes wonna play with babies huh? Well, look what we did to yours." I said as I grabbed her in a handful of her weave and drug her across the kitchen floor into the living room.

She cried and begged me to stop and said she didn't know where Amira was as I continued to drag her and punch her ass in the face. When we got back to where we had left her children I threw her right on top of her oldest son and daughter, both missing a face.

"Oh nooooo. Please. I don't know where she at. Oh, no Quatty. You rotten bastard. I hope she kill that little bitch. Oh my God." Lay Lay yelled as I hit her with my gun so hard and so many times, blood splattered everywhere.

She was barely conscious when Ghost drug her son back into the room and I yanked him up in the air by his neck.

"Tell me where she at you bitch and I'll spare this little faggot. Otherwise I make you watch me gut his bitch ass and paint the walls with his blood. The choice is yours hoe, but you better hurry up because my arm getting tired." I said as Durty laughed and yanked that bloody bitch up to her knees.

"Tell him now bitch or he ain't gonna have to kill him because I will. And in the most painful way possible too." Durty said as Lay Lay got hysterical.

I could see her break before our eyes as she reached out for my feet and begged me not to kill her son.

"Okay, Quatty please. Just don't kill him. I don't really know where she at but I know she in east Memphis. I know that because my friend that works at Superlo on Winchester called about ten minutes ago saying Pooh was in the store buying a cooler and ice and got into it with a customer. Supposedly some girl somebody called Yada beat her ass and shot at her on the lot. They say Pooh got away though when some good Samaritans jumped in. So, I told you all I know now Quatty. Just let him go." Lay Lay said gasping as I laughed at her.

There she was, the rotten bitch who had helped to kill my baby and destroy everything I worked for, begging for mercy. The audacity of that bitch to ever expect anything in life other than the hurt she had put out. She had me fucked up though because good Quatty was lost for the moment, all that was left was the beast. Without saying another word, I raised my hand with my gun in it, put it to her son head, and blew his brains out. I made sure to dangle his lifeless body over her head so that blood could rain down on her as she cried.

"Yeah bitch his blood is on your hands." I yelled as I threw his body at her then walked to the door.

At the door, I stopped and looked back as I told Ghost to give me a cigarette. He looked puzzled as he handed it to me and a lighter then asked was I okay.

"Almost my nigga, almost. Just trying to figure out where the bitch at. I got an idea though. Aye Durty, have some fun with that bitch. You got three minutes let's see how much damage you can do." I said as Ghost shook his head and laughed and I lit my cigarette.

That was all I had to say as Durty laid his massive hands on Lay Lay in the worse way. After four punches to the face and head her muffled screams stopped and I had to walk out on to the porch to finish my cigarette because the beating was so brutal. I had no sympathy for her or what she was going through, I just didn't want to see that shit. I stood there for a minute and smoked before Ghost came out and told me it was done.

"Ain't shit left of that bitch but hair, and not much of that either. That nigga a beast for real, so now it's off to Pooh." Ghost said as I nodded my head, flicked my cigarette, and stepped off the porch.

Ghost whistled and called all the homies and they came out from their posts just as Durty came out the house. I looked back just as we made it to the cars and saw the flicker of flames dancing inside.

"Never leave a trace." Durty said after he saw what I was looking at then I nodded my head.

I gave that nigga dap as we all stood in the shadows around the truck and shed all of our clothes. We gave shoes, clothes, and guns to Durty before I handed out the black jogging suits me and Ghost had brought and brand new Nikes to boot. Once we were all dressed I handed out orders ready to get gone.

"Aite, we know the hoe in the east but not the exact location. Y'all niggas go to her cousin house in the Belle Vista and kill everybody there. You know what my baby and Pooh look like so if you see them call me before you do anything to Pooh. Secure my princess though and guard her with your life. Durty, you go to that bitch brother house and do what you do best. After that, get rid of the steamer, guns, and clothes then disappear. Durty, you know where to meet us, you and Yada gone get that head start. Peedy, if you and Twala still down y'all welcome to go so you gonna have about thirty minutes to be behind us after this shit goes down. Y'all Niggas." I said turning to the homies who had come to help.

"Y'all niggas got loot already in them bags. Check the truck and you will see. This shit never happened and you never saw us in Memphis. Once we gone we gone, so love folk. Y'all niggas came through." I said before I shook them up then me and Ghost got in the truck, crunk up, and pulled out.

We got back to Memphis faster than we left and once we got in East Memphis Peedy nem went towards Belle Vista and I was drawn towards our old house. Even though I knew that damn near the whole street was condemned after a string of fires, something was still telling me to hit that block and check it out. I didn't ignore that voice that time and as soon as I pulled on the block and saw a flicker of a dull light through one of the semi-bordered up windows of our old house, I knew Pooh was there.

"Fool that bitch in there, I'm going to get my baby." I said after I parked on the street and started to get out. Ghost grabbed my arm and told me to wait as I turned to look at him.

"Wait fool, we don't know who in there with the bitch. Let me call the crew." Ghost said as he dialed Peedy's number and I got out of the truck anyway.

When I got out I instantly got a chill and it wasn't because of the night air. The muffled cries of a little girl was what made the hair on the back of my neck stand up and my heart beat out of control.

"Fuck that, tell Peedy to go home and get his shit then wait on us. Call the girls and tell them to head to Peedy's house and get ready to go. I got this you can come cover my back, but I'm going to get my baby regardless." I said as I cocked my gun and ran up on to the porch.

I could see the taillights and backend of a blue house from the porch which was parked in the bushes. That was all that I needed to see to kick that fucking door off the hinges. As soon as that bitch flew open I rushed in to the dark stanky ass living room. I could see nothing inside as I walked forward, nothing but a little dim candle light coming from the bathroom.

I walked in with my gun up and aimed as I stumbled over shit but I was too focused to see what it was. I made it half way down the hall before Ghost suddenly appeared in the door and pulled his phone out of his pocket. I put my finger up to my lips to tell him to be quiet as I heard muffled cries and scratches from behind the half-opened bathroom door. My adrenaline kicked in right at that moment and I kicked that bitch on open just as Ghost flashed the light from his phone on the living room and yelled out my name.

I wasn't hearing him though because I was standing there looking at the fucking devil. There was Pooh looking dirty and deranged as she sat on top of a cooler with blood all over her hands and face. She laughed and clapped her hands when she saw me standing there, completely out of her mind.

"You slow ass bitch." I yelled as I shot that hoe in the chest and she flew into the tub.

I ran over and untied the rope she had around the cooler as she moaned and laughed while she spit out blood.

"It's too late Quatty, she dead. She long gone by now. I bet that bitch wasn't worth that was she." Pooh said as she laughed and I ignored her while I ripped the lid off the cooler.

I just knew Amira wasn't dead even though when I opened the cooler I saw it was filled with bloody water and my baby was face down in it. I stood there for a second and watched her take short, shallow breaths just like I had taught her many times in our pool. What Pooh didn't know was that my baby was already a future Olympian and could swim better than Michael Felts. Amira could hold her breath for almost two minutes and then take shallow enough breaths for three additional minutes to appear dead. I had trained my baby to be a soldier and she didn't even know it. That's why my heart wasn't aching as much when I reached in and pulled out her little limp, wet body out of the water.

"Amira, its daddy. Open your eyes princess. I love you more than a King loves all of his riches. Why? Because nothing is worth more than a princess or a Queen." I said and my baby's eyes fluttered open and she looked directly at me.

"Daddy." Amira cried as I held her tightly in my arms and ran my fingers across the bleeding gash in her forehead.

Pooh laughed and cursed as I held her and with blood on my hands I turned to look at the bitch.

"Bitch your blood gonna be on my hands next." I said to her before I yelled out Ghost's name.

In seconds he was standing in the doorway stiff as a board and as white as his name. I didn't bother to ask him what was wrong as I handed him Amira and then hopped straight on Pooh's ass. I beat that bitch like one of Denise's kids, from a book called Sins of Thy Mother as I released all of that anger I had held for years.

"You rotten bitch. Stupid ass hoe. You just couldn't let go. You made me murder you. Hoe I hate you with you stanky ass. Die maggot ass hoe." I said after I had beat her face to a pulp and wrapped my hands around her neck.

I choked until I felt all of her bones crack then I got up, grabbed my gun off the floor, and shot her in the head three times. I was still angry after that just thinking about what she tried to do so I ran back over there and stomped that bitch until my leg started to ache. I was in such a hateful daze I could hear or see nothing around me. Ghost brought me out of it when he grabbed my shoulder and screamed my name to tell me Amira passed out.

"What? What happened?" I asked as I suddenly stopped and ran over to take her out of his arms.

Ghost cried like a baby as he handed her to me then led us out the house with the light from his phone. That time when I walked through the living room I could see what was lying in the floor. There in the darkness in puddles of blood was Pooh's three kids. Seeing them laying there, the kids I vowed to protect, I broke down and damn near got weak in the knees. The unconscious moans of my own daughter brought me out of it though as I continued to cry while I ran out the house.

I jumped in the car with my baby in my arms and Ghost got in the driver's seat as I took out my phone and called Tinka. I told her I had Amira and was headed to Delta Medical, and she said she was right by there. I told her when we got there she had to get the baby and take her in and to say she fell, hit her head then rolled in the pool. Tinka told me okay and that she loved me before we hung up. When we pulled up two minutes later the ladies were already there and I kissed my baby before I handed her off.

"We going get cleaned up and get rid of the truck then I'll be back. Just remember the story and tell Amira before they ask her anything." I told Tinka as she nodded then kissed me before she ran inside.

I kissed and hugged Lilly as Ghost kissed belle then we got in the truck and left. When we got back downtown to Peedy's shop everyone was waiting to see what had happened. I got out with tears in my eyes and a smile on my face and they all knew what went down.

"I knew we would get her back now time to go." Peedy said as we went to work.

Peedy told me how they killed all of Pooh's cousins and Lay Lay's brother and Durty finished the mother as we got cleaned up and sent the homies away with the cars. It was an hour after I found my baby so I called Tinka and she told me Amira was ok.

"They said it was just a minor cut, but head wounds bleed. We are being discharged now so we will be ready when you get here." Tinka said as I heard the relief in her voice.

I told her how much I loved them all and I how sorry I was before I hung up the phone.

"It's all over y'all Amira is okay. Now it's time to start over. Let's get the fuck out of Memphis because we know Johnny Law coming." I said as my niggas agreed and we loaded up to leave.

Ghost and I got back into the truck and Peedy and Twala got into their truck which was loaded with their most prized possessions. They were going to Bora Bora with us so as I drove back to the hospital to get the girls I called L and got his pilot ready for us to take that private flight. He said we could leave by two the next afternoon and I told him we would be there.

"Aite, everything straight. L got us a private plane but its big as fuck so everybody can go. We can only take a little clothes and important paper work but we will start all over where we're going. So now all we gotta do is get the girls, get home, and wait till the bank open so we can catch the flight. Then we can leave all this bullshit behind." I said as I drove towards the hospital and finally, some real peace.

We picked up the girls and hit the road anxious to get the fuck away. I couldn't help but to look in the rearview mirror every thirty seconds expecting the police to be on our ass. They weren't though and we made it back to Charlotte just a little after nine that morning. Everyone was tired as hell when we got there but there was no time for rest. I had been checking Memphis news periodically throughout the ride so I knew the police were looking for me for questioning. Someone had told the police they saw me in Memphis so naturally I was the first suspect. They had me fucked up though because there was no way in hell I was going back to jail.

I jumped out as soon as I parked in the driveway and grabbed my baby out and into my arms. I cried and hugged and kissed her all the way into the house before I handed her to Sasha and told her to get Amira ready. She did exactly what I said and ran upstairs with my baby in her arms as I lead Tinka and Lilly upstairs. I could hear Durty and Yada come through the door as we made it to the top and I yelled out welcome to their new home. I had decided to sign the house over to him and leave him all the dope. Moe was cool with that after I told him what I had planned so I was doing it with a lean conscious.

Durty yelled out thank you as I told him to go hide it far from the house and he went to go get it. I went into the master bath and turned on the shower as Tinka and Lilly shed their clothing and then I did the same thing. We all stepped in and took a silent, quick shower as we cried and held one another. Once the shower was over it was all out of our systems so we hopped straight back to business. Lilly dressed in the business suit I had gotten for her and put on the blonde wig so she would look just like the Lillian on the ID. After that Tinka and I dressed then we made our way downstairs where everyone was waiting.

"Okay this is it. Let' go crew." I said as my ladies hugged Yada and Yada said how much she loved us.

"After we take this city by storm, we'll be out there to visit, maybe even stay. Love y'all though, stay safe." Yada said as we rushed out of the house as Durty pulled back up.

I showed my nigga love before I told him everything he needed to know then hopped in the truck. I took one last look at the mansion we had loved and grown in before I blew my horn to tell Lilly, Tinka, and Belle we were about to pull out. Tinka blew back then I pulled out with Peedy, Ghost, and the kids riding with me. We followed them into downtown Charlotte and parked across the street from the bank. I was anxious as fuck from the time they walked in, scared something would go wrong.

After five minutes I had my gun in hand ready to go in that bitch and get them out. Peedy stopped me though as he pointed to the door so that I would look. There was my girls, Lilly and Tinka, coming out of the bank with four big bags in their hands. I watched them pull off and get halfway down the street before I yelled out in joy and my niggas joined in. It felt good as hell knowing what they had so much so I don't even remember pulling away from the curb I was so high on happiness. I do remember looking back when we got about six blocks down and seeing the police pull up in front of the bank.

That shit made my heart race and I pushed my car to 80 as I told Peedy to call the girls and tell them to get there now and Ghost to call L and tell him to have the pilot ready right then. I got confirmation on both cars as I turned the corner away from the air strip and saw freedom and happiness within my reach. I drove like a damn Nascar driver up the long road next to the airstrip and barely stopped before I swung my door open and jumped out. Tinka and the girls were already there unloaded, and standing on the steps of the plane when I began pulling the little kids out the truck and sending them over to them.

We got everyone out in two minutes and boarded the plane ready to go. I could barely stop my heart from racing as I yelled for the pilot to go while I kept my eyes out the window looking for the cops. I spotted them bitches too a few blocks away as the flashed their lights. It was too late at that point though because we were already going down the runway headed to freedom. I finally sighed and let my head fall back on to the seat a couple of minutes later when we finally began to ascend into the sky.

I looked down at the minute police cars as they pulled into the airstrip and waved goodbye. That was the last I saw of Memphis, Pooh, or any unhappiness for that matter. Every day after that was sunshine and happiness in Bora Bora with the two women who loved me most. I found out the hard way that every bitch wasn't worth it, but in the end that lesson lead me to the happiest times of my life. When it was all said and done...Tinka was worth it!

Sneak Peek of…

# I Hope She's Worth It 3: Shawty My Shoota
## A Durty & Yada Kinda Love

## Prologue

Loud bangs on the front door jolted me up off the couch and on my feet. I looked over at Yada as she quickly ran up the stairs and I went towards the door. The bangs continued as I walked closer and glanced back to see Yada standing on the top step as she whispered there was dope in the house. I told her to get rid of it as I walked closer to the damn door and she ran back up. I had told her ass to get the dope we brought with us out of the house as soon as Quatty nem left, but in true hard headed ass Yada fashion, she ignored me. Just like always she let her need to do what the fuck she wanted to do cloud her judgement.

My bitch was so much of a goon, she just really had no chill. People thought I was the hot-headed ass beast, but in reality, Yada was a hundred times more vicious then me. She just hid her crazy with a pretty face and dope ass body. That didn't change the fact that her fuck up was about to cause me my freedom though. I already knew it was Charlotte Police at the door looking for Quatty nem and that they would take my big, black, ex-convict ass as a consolation prize if they couldn't find their marks. That's exactly why I didn't plan on opening that bitch at all. I was going to let them bitches continue knocking until they finally gave up. That wasn't in cards though and I found that out as soon as them bitches started kicking the door in.

"Charlotte Police Department. We have a search warrant open the damn door." An officer yelled as I smirked at the door like he had lost his damn mind and ran towards the left wing to where I stashed my 40.

I was ready to have a shoot out and show them bitches just how determined I was not to go back to jail. I yelled up to Yada, telling her to get out of the house because I wasn't going back as she yelled back that she wouldn't. I grabbed my 40 from the vase in the hall just inside the left wing before I dashed back out and towards the steps. I was on my way upstairs to make Yada ass disappear to the panic room Quatty told me was there and order her to stay until I was dead or back in jail. However, I didn't get a chance to get there because right before I could get up two steps them mutha fuckas were barging in with guns drawn yelling for me to get on my knees.

"Freeze, put your hands in the air. Are you Quaderious Jones?" They asked as I continued to stand on the steps frozen with my gun in hand.

The police continued to yell commands as I stood there and thought about what I should do. That killer, greater side of me wanted to turn around bussing but I was unsure on how many of them bitches were behind me. That's why I listened to my weak side and simply put my hands up. When them bitches saw the gun in my hand they panicked like a muthafucka and before I knew it had 12, 000 jolts of electricity surging through my ass.

I fell backwards down the stairs damn near paralyzed and looked up into the faces of the two, rookie, weak ass cops who had come to serve that search warrant. Them bitches didn't look qualified or even ready for the action they were about to see. I had no time to warn them though as I suddenly heard my bitch began to laugh and I joined in with her. Both of the cops stood up straight with guns in hand and searched around for the laughter. They searched all over downstairs but never got a glimpse of Yada.

By the time they did see her it was too late though as my bitch popped up out of the huge picture hanging on the wall by the front door, which was really one of the entrances to the panic room and tunnels below. Yada had gone into the panic room upstairs' entrance when I said it and I guess she watched shit go down on the cameras from there. When she saw they bitches taser me, my bitch did what she does best and that's eliminate all threats. She came up through them tunnels like a fucking monster and rattled them bitch ass cops right off their square. Three minutes after the laughter began they were still looking around, searching for the source.

"Call back up." The young black one said as he looked at me and I continued to laugh and shake my head.

I could feel the temporary paralysis from the taser starting to wear off as I continued to look at the cop and he wondered what I meant. He didn't wonder long though because the next thing he knew a bullet was flying through the air and straight into his eye. That muthafucka fell like a box of rocks as brains and blood flew everywhere.

I got my baring's back and stumbled to my feet just as the other cop began to return fire wildly in every direction. I took a bullet to the left leg that went in and out as I tried to make it over to my gun. That bitch threw me off balance too as I fell to my knees and the cop continued to shoot. Three bullets later, I thought my ass was dead but when the smoke cleared I saw my baby standing in the corner by the door behind the grandfather clock with her still smoking strap in hand.

"I got them bitches, now get up baby. We gotta get the fuck out of here. Good we didn't bring much cause we gotta go." Yada said as she pulled me up then bent down to examine my leg.

"It went in and out so you good. I'll get you fixed up when we get outside of the city safely. Right now, we gonna head to the dope and money you buried then straight out of town. That was a close call that time though. I thought that lil bitch would kill you. Ole faggot ass." Yada said as she put two more bullets in the cops head before she helped me out the door.

I got in the car and fired up a Newport as I watched Yada sprint back into the house and quickly clean up the scene. My baby was like a muthafucking assassin working alone, quick and efficient. That bitch had saved me so many times I had lost count, and got me in shit so many times too. At the end of the day though, she was worth it all because nobody rode for me like she did.

"Shawty you my shoota for real and nothing will ever take what we have. It's a Durty and Yada kinda love until the day they judge us by 12 or bury us by six." I said to my baby once she jumped back into the car and told me we were set to go.

"You better believe it baby. I love you Durty." Yada said as we sped out of the yard and towards our first lick.

# PEN HUSTLAS PUBLICATIONS

PEN HUSTLAS IS TAKING SUBMISSIONS IN ALL GENRES. IF YOU WOULD LIKE TO BE A PART OF OUR TEAM, PLEASE SEND YOUR SUBMISSIONS BY EMAIL TO PENHUSTLASPUBLICATIONS@GMAIL.COM PLEASE INCLUDE A BRIEF BIO, A SYNOPSIS OF THE BOOK, AND THE FIRST FOUR THREE CHAPTERS. SUBMIT USING MICROSOFT WORD WITH FONT IN 11 TIMES NEW ROMAN.

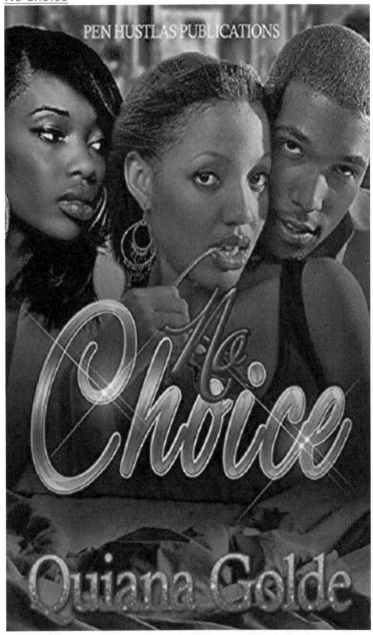

PEN HUSTLAS PUBLICATIONS

No Choice

Quiana Golde

Made in the USA
Columbia, SC
19 August 2017